Sierra Oscar Sierra

KELLY UTT

STANDARDS
OF STARLIGHT

2024 Standards of Starlight Paperback Edition

www.standardsofstarlight.com

Cover art by Elizabeth Mackey

ISBN: 978-1-952893-31-5

Preface

"It is the secret of the world that all things subsist and do not die, but only retire a little from sight and afterwards return again. Nothing is dead. Men feign themselves dead, and endure mock funerals and mournful obituaries, and there they stand looking out of the window, sound and well, in some strange new disguise."

—Ralph Waldo Emerson

Prologue

SIERRA

They say you know when you're about to die. The world slows, the air thickens, and suddenly, every moment stretches like a rubber band pulled to its breaking point. The transition is, supposedly, pleasant. Like jumping into a cool swimming pool on a hot day.

But that's not how it happened for me.

For me, it was a flash. A flicker of light, a jolt of pain, and ... nothing.

When I opened my eyes, everything was just as I'd left it. The sun was shining, the birds were singing, and the scent of fresh coffee lingered in the air. Life, as it seemed, went on.

But something wasn't right. The shadows were too sharp, the colors too bright. The air felt heavy, like I was breathing through a thick, invisible fog. And then there was Oscar—my Oscar. He'd been so different. Distant. As if he were looking right through me, seeing something I couldn't.

"I'm here," I whispered, reaching out to touch him. But my hand passed through his shoulder like smoke. He didn't flinch. Didn't even blink.

A cold dread curled in my stomach, twisting tighter with every heartbeat. No, not heartbeats. There was no pulse, no warmth, and no life. Only an echo. A ghost of what used to be.

I stumbled backward, my mind spinning, grasping for logic in the madness. Deep down, I already knew the truth. I could feel it. A hollow emptiness where life used to be.

I was dead.

But this wasn't the end.

It was just the beginning.

PART ONE
Wolf of Virginia

Chapter One

SIERRA

One Week Earlier

"He isn't the same," I say forcefully as I swing my foot under the metal table. "Not since the helo crash."

I'm wearing modest brown heels and a blue pencil skirt that stretches below my knees. A crisp white blouse is tucked beneath a gray sweater I bought yesterday at the sprawling mall just west of the base. My long, chestnut-colored hair is pulled back into a tight ponytail. I hope I'm dressed appropriately for the occasion. I also hope it isn't presumptuous to use military jargon like the word helo.

"What do you mean?" the gentleman asks. "Of course, he's the same. Captain Teague is your husband. He's the man you married."

As if Oscar's relationship to me makes this any better. It doesn't. In fact, it makes it worse.

I'm the one stuck with him during his down time, when he finally comes home for a little while because the Marine

Corps doesn't have anything pressing for him to do. I'm the one he takes his frustrations out on when the brass tells him to get some rest and relaxation, since my husband apparently no longer understands the meaning of either word. And I'm the one running out of options. This isn't the wedded bliss I expected when I put my own life and career on hold to follow Oscar Teague to a top-secret duty station in Quantico, Virginia.

We live in nearby Woodbridge, but that's hardly relevant to anyone but me at this point. In his mind and heart, Oscar is always right here, at Marine Corps Base Quantico.

"I'm telling you, something isn't right. Oscar is *different*," I try. "He most certainly is *not* the man I married. Far from it. And I believe you know why. The real question is, will you reveal what you know?"

I'm nervous, and I'm sure it shows.

I try to keep my voice calm. Even. I silently command my foot to be still. It cooperates, reluctantly. Less than a minute later, though, my hands find each other and I begin clicking my fingernails together at a fast tempo. They make a sound loud enough to be heard across the room. I can tell because the young blonde assistant in the corner glances up from her paperwork to give me a dirty look. She did the same in response to my foot swinging.

"What?" I ask.

Isn't that the way life goes? A nuisance stops, only to be replaced by another in one endless stream of irritations.

The assistant is young. Younger than me, anyway. She'll learn.

The girl—all I can bring myself to call her—pauses long enough to make her point, then turns back to her neat stack of papers. She's probably taking notes on what I say. She wants to be useful to her superiors, I'm sure. And hey, I hear that Women Marines have a harder time earning respect than females in other branches of the military. I should probably give this girl a break. She smooths the front of her uniform before spreading her palms flat across the tiny desk she's been assigned. I can tell she's trying to focus. My nervousness is distracting her.

"Whatever," I mumble under my breath.

She isn't worth the energy. I have other—more important—things on my mind. And I'm running out of time to express my concerns. I doubt Brigadier General Carl Benedict will take long out of his busy schedule for me. He's an influential guy who has swarms of people vying for his attention. Truth be told, I'm surprised to have gotten this far with him. I had better not push my luck.

"Ms. Mallory ..."

"Dr. Mallory," I correct.

It's been less than two years since I graduated with my PhD in clinical psychology from Emory University, but that title was hard earned. I won't let the slight pass.

"Of course. My apologies, Dr. Mallory."

I nod approvingly.

General Benedict does the same, then smoothes the hair on the side of his head as he thinks. He motions in a wide sweep, his thumb trailing over his ear and his palm following. His dark hair is cut so short that I'm not sure what he hopes to smooth. It reminds me of an amputee grasping for a missing limb.

And he thinks I'm delusional.

This man could grow his hair long if he so chose. Only

the Marine Corps wouldn't allow it. He'd have to abandon his post, throw away his career, and start an entirely new life, just to satisfy his inclination to tuck a few strands behind his ears. So, here he is, a decorated military officer, forced to smooth hair that isn't actually there.

"Dr. Mallory?" he asks.

"Yes?"

"I suppose I don't understand what you mean when you say that Captain Teague is different. If I didn't know better, Dr. Mallory, I'd say your concern sounds like it's in regard to what can only be described as a private, domestic situation. One that the Marine Corps would have no business being involved in."

He smirks as he says it. He's already dismissing me. Being addressed as doctor was a hollow victory.

That bastard.

Frustration builds behind what I hope is still a composed, serious expression on my face. I'm well aware that this isn't the time to get emotional, but I'm finding it hard to hold my true feelings back. I came here because I thought I had no other choice. I guess I expected a warmer welcome and more concern for Oscar. Whatever is wrong with him, it's the Marine Corps' fault. It has to be. Like I said, at a minimum, they know something about it.

Maybe my husband was exposed to something during an overseas mission? As a military intelligence officer, he travels around the globe on a regular basis. A physical illness might explain the changes in his behavior. Or maybe he was put under so much stress that he experienced some sort of mental break.

I may be a psychologist, but I'm not supposed to diagnose

family members. The American Psychological Association has strict rules about that sort of thing. I'd be in violation of ethics guidelines and my career would be over before it had even begun if I tried. And besides, I don't have enough information to properly diagnose him. I'd need to see a full medical workup plus gain access to any mental health records that the military might have on file. Perhaps this isn't the first time Oscar has exhibited concerning behavioral changes. I'm not sure he would have sought help, though. The Marine Corps frowns on mental health issues being brought to light, especially for officers in high pressure positions like Oscar's.

All of that leaves me exactly nowhere.

"General Benedict, respectfully, what would you like me to do about the *situation*?" I ask. "If I'd thought I could handle it on my own, I wouldn't be sitting here in front of you right now. I know how busy you are, sir. I don't take this lightly."

He eyes me skeptically, one brow raising high on his forehead. He seems to appreciate my deference to his authority, and I make a mental note of that. I'll surely need to use the tactic again. I honestly do respect the man. From everything Oscar has told me, Carl is one of the truly good guys. It's why I chose to reach out to him first.

Carl takes a deep breath and I avert my gaze, looking out the narrow window on the wall behind his desk. I remain still, giving him another minute to think things over.

It's late February, and the day is foggy and gray, meeting my mood. I suppose I ought to expect as much from Northern Virginia this time of year.

It's been sixteen months since I moved north from Atlanta. I still miss the mild Georgia winters. There, it's currently warming up as March approaches. Flowers are coming into bloom, average temperatures are climbing, and the sun shines brightly on most days. I wish I was in Atlanta right now, in fact. It would be a hell of a lot better than this depressing gloom. More accurately, I wish I could go back and do something else that would land us in a better place—both figuratively and literally. I fear coming to Quantico was a huge, life-altering mistake.

"Dr. Mallory," Carl begins anew, coming around to my side. "Please, if you will, tell me more. How *exactly* is Captain Teague different?"

"I'm glad you asked," I reply, scooting to the front edge of my seat and placing my hands on the edge of Carl's desk. His eyes flick down at them. I've overstepped. I quickly remove my hands, folding them in my lap. "Sorry," I say. I hate apologizing.

"Go on," he says with a nod.

The blonde girl in the corner eyes me eagerly, a pen balanced in one of her hands, ready to take more notes. It strikes me as odd that she doesn't appear to be typing. Who takes handwritten notes these days? Maybe it's a military thing. I don't know, but I wish she wasn't here and that Carl and I were alone. I don't like the thought of this discussion being on the record, filed away forevermore.

"Is it possible ... for us to be alone?" I try.

Except that didn't come out right. Now I probably sound like a harlot. Like I'm trying to seduce the general or something.

Not a good look. I suck in my pride and try again.

"I mean, might we have some privacy?" I clarify. "I'd feel more comfortable if what we say here today isn't recorded."

Carl hunches his shoulders as if he's exasperated by me. He seems to be flipping back and forth. One minute, he's sympathetic to my cause and appears to be thinking about helping me. The next, he's righteously pissed off and might throw me out of his office. I'm not sure I'm worth that much of an exaggerated response, but I persist.

"If it isn't too much trouble," I add. "I'll keep it short."

"Fine," Carl concedes.

He waves the assistant out without making eye contact. She furrows her brow, inclined to protest, but she thinks better of it. In a flurry of shuffling papers and shuffling feet, she's gone. The door closes hard behind her, and Carl and I are left alone. His demeanor softens the moment our eyes meet.

Thank goodness.

I was introduced to Carl and his wife, Rita, at an event at the Officer's Club on base once. He'd been relaxed then, probably thanks to some warm liquor and the feeling of his lovely lady in his hands as they glided across the dance floor together. I suspect the familiarity that encounter garnered is a large part of why the General agreed to see me today. I search my memories from the evening for something I can mention that will help lower his defenses now. I keep my facial expression fixed as I comb through my mind behind the scenes.

I could mention the food that was served. Tapping into a sensory memory sounds promising. Mentioning the music might be an even better choice. If I'm lucky, and the song I mention ties into another memory for Carl, then he'll definitely let his guard down. How to choose?

I quickly think through the songs he and Rita danced to, then I try to extrapolate which might have the most powerful emotional connections. I base the probability of a high emotional response on the approximate year the song first came out as compared to Carl's age. I also consider his reaction to the song.

Yes, that's good. I'm on the right track.

I remember the couple dancing a little closer when Van Morrison's *Brown Eyed Girl* came on. That song was released in the late sixties. Carl and Rita aren't old enough to have been adults then, but their parents are. Maybe Carl listened to the song as a kid. It's worth a shot. As best I can remember, the other songs they danced to were relatively new. I doubt Ed Sheeran or John Legend would mean as much.

I swallow hard and give it a go.

"General, I remember the night you and I met. I couldn't help but notice you holding your wife close—the same way Oscar held me—when *Brown Eyed Girl* came on. It's clear you love Rita very much."

"That, I do," he replies.

As he speaks, he softens again, more completely this time. If I look only at his face and ignore the uniform below, Carl could be any other friendly guy you'd expect to find at a dog park, a grocery store, or a cozy family restaurant. He's human in there, for sure. I imagine you don't get to his rank and position without having a soft side to balance out the required intensity.

I say a silent prayer that Carl's soft side will win out today.

"I love Oscar very much," I say. "If you will, sir, please put yourself in my shoes for a moment. My beloved husband has a dangerous job. One that sees him in harm's way more often than I probably realize."

His eyes droop ever so slightly at the edges. He's sympathizing with me.

"And then one day, he returns home after having been in a helicopter crash. At first, I'm incredibly relieved that he's safe and that he returned to me in one piece. But I'm telling you, the man who walked into our home that day is an entirely different one than the Oscar Teague who left the month before. He feels like ... a stranger. A stranger in my arms. A stranger in bed ..."

The general shifts his weight. I've made him uncomfortable now.

Yet I press on.

"Imagine that, sir. Wouldn't you be horrified if Rita was suddenly different in the most intimate ways? If you could sense at a fundamental level that your spouse wasn't the person you knew and loved?"

He breathes deeply.

"Dr. Mallory, of course, I love my wife. And I don't doubt you love your husband. But frankly, you're not giving me much to work with. I need specifics if I'm to do anything at all to help you. Otherwise ..."

"Oscar can't always get an erection anymore," I blurt.

The general's eyes open wide as if he's scandalized. Surely, he's heard and seen all kinds of worse things. Haven't all military men? Scratch that. Haven't all men of a certain age?

"He's angry all the time. He drives dangerously fast. He's short with me, and with his mother. He doesn't sleep at night. He stopped tending his herb garden. He ..."

"Perhaps he should see a medical doctor for a diagnosis," Carl tries. "None of the things you mention sound like any concern of mine."

"He has trouble finding words," I continue. "He won't eat his favorite foods. It's as if suddenly, he doesn't fit into his own life or environment."

I seem to have his attention now. He leans forward, peering into my eyes.

"Does he seriously have trouble finding words?"

"Yes!" I say. "Have you spent any time around him lately?"

Carl shakes his head, then pulls a pen and a pad of paper from his desk drawer.

"Not much. Captain Teague and I don't have occasion to work together often these days. I see him in the building. We wave and smile, but that's about the extent of it. He doesn't look any different."

I lean forward, too, meeting Carl's heightened level of interest. I'm grateful for the glimmer of hope I'm feeling.

"Call him in," I say. "Spend fifteen minutes with Oscar. Ask a few pointed questions. I think you'll see what I mean."

I nod, confirming the suggestion and prompting Carl to act on it.

"Now?"

"No time like the present, sir," I say.

There's so much more I want to say, but I hold back. Step one is convincing the general that Oscar has a problem. Once that door is open, I'll share more information. I've been taking notes and compiling a list of oddities. My training as a psychologist has definitely helped me in that department. I'm all over the data.

"Done," Carl says, and I appreciate his ability to make decisions quickly. "Give me a little time. Within a week, I'll be ready to either talk about this more or put the subject to rest once and for all. Sound fair?"

General Benedict stands. I shoot out of my chair as if I must stand at attention and salute, but I stop myself short. I nod enthusiastically instead, then shove my hand towards him for a shake.

"Thank you, sir," I say. "You're a lifesaver."

Chapter Two

OSCAR

I'm tired of being badgered.

Sometimes, I think Sierra forgets who I am. Maybe I'm not the man she married, but who is? We all change.

Hell, marriage changes you in ways no one can prepare you for. The moment the vows are exchanged, something unspoken shifts. There are new responsibilities, expectations, and rules of engagement that aren't written down anywhere. God knows I've tried to follow them. But no one told me that a single event could cost me my soul, shape-shifting it into something unrecognizable even to the closest person in my life, her. If that's what's even happening.

The helicopter crash changed everything. Nothing I'd experienced up to that point in my life begins to compare.

I wish I'd been somewhere else that day instead of God-forsaken Afghanistan. I wish something—anything—had intervened so that life would have left me as I was. I was doing fine. My existence was good.

When it happened, the sound was deafening. The rotors

above screamed as they fought against the impossible, slicing through the air with a fury that rattled my bones. I could feel the vibrations deep in my chest. The thrum was relentless. Everything around me was chaos—lights flashing, alarms blaring, voices shouting, but none of it made sense.

We were going down. I knew it the second the chopper shuddered violently, a jolt so fierce it nearly threw me from my seat. Instinct kicked in, and my training took over. My hands moved on their own, gripping the harness, tightening it, securing myself as if that would make any difference.

"Brace! Brace! Brace!" The pilot's voice cut through the noise, sharp and desperate.

My body tensed, muscles coiling like springs, every nerve on edge. I could see the ground spinning up towards us, a blur of brown and green, too fast, too close.

The trees that had looked so small from above now loomed like giants, ready to tear us apart.

Time slowed. The seconds stretched out, each one an eternity as the Earth rushed up to meet us. I heard the rotors scream one last time, a high-pitched wail of metal on metal, before everything went white. There was no pain, just a blinding light and a sensation of weightlessness, like I was suspended in midair, caught between life and death.

Then, there was the impact.

It was like nothing I'd ever felt before—a force that tore through the helicopter, through me, like a bomb going off inside my skull. The sound was indescribable. It was a cacophony of breaking glass, twisting metal, and the terrible, gut-wrenching crunch as we hit the ground. My body jerked violently, the harness cutting into my chest, my shoulders. I tasted blood, felt the sharp sting of something slicing across my face.

And then, there was silence.

For a moment, I thought I was dead. Everything was so still and quiet, like the world had stopped.

I couldn't move. Couldn't breathe. All I could do was stare at the wreckage around me, the twisted remains of the chopper, the bodies—God, the bodies—strewn across the ground like broken dolls.

I lost friends that day.

Pain came in waves, crashing over me and threatening to pull me under. My head throbbed and my vision blurred. I tried to move, but my body wouldn't respond. Everything felt wrong, like I was disconnected.

Somewhere in the distance, I heard voices—shouts, footsteps, the crackle of a radio. But they felt miles away. I wanted to call out, to tell them I was here, but my mouth wouldn't work.

And then, there was darkness. It came swiftly, wrapping around me and pulling me under. I didn't fight it. I couldn't. I was so tired, so damn tired.

As I slipped away, one thought cut through the haze, clear and sharp: *I'm not going to make it out of this.*

And then there was nothing.

By some miracle, I was stabilized at Bagram Airfield and then transported to Landstuhl Regional Medical Center in Germany. It was nearly a month before I was well enough to go home and back to Sierra.

I shake off the thought as I punch the code into the door that leads to the isolated wing of the base, trying to focus.

Work keeps me grounded—or at least it used to. If I could just dive into some new briefing, analyze intel reports, or tackle anything that requires me to laser-cut my attention with precision, maybe then I'd stop feeling this way. Like a foreign entity is crawling under my skin, pulling all the strings.

Sometimes, I feel like a marionette gone rogue. Hands, mind—and let's not even talk about the heart—all seem to be operating under some fucked-up program I didn't install.

FUBAR. That's what us jarheads call Fucked Up Beyond All Repair.

The room inside isn't much better than the corridor outside—a sterile box with fluorescent lighting as garish and unforgiving as my old drill sergeant at Parris Island. But it's secure. I throw my bag into the corner and scrub at my face, almost as though I can wash away everything Sierra said this morning. All her questions, her eyes searching mine like she could solve whatever puzzle she thinks I've become if she just stares hard enough.

Something in me flinches, recoiling from the thought of returning home. With her. It's crazy, but the sensation spreads through me like cracks in glass, swallowing my control inch by inch, and I don't know how to stop it.

More than anything, I just want to forget.

Forget my wife's prying eyes. Forget the way she looks at me now, like my skin is some text she could read, and I'm hiding footnotes from her. Forget how she reminds me that I'm a malfunctioning part in some well-oiled machine.

I'm a person, damn it. Even if I don't feel like one these days.

I hear a knock on the door, soft at first, then more insistent. My body reacts before my mind can catch up—a trained response, some reflex buried deep in my muscle memory. I straighten, wiping any trace of inner turmoil from my face, and unlock the door.

"Captain Teague," a voice greets me, professional and firm.

It's General Benedict, standing in full uniform, his eyes boring into mine with an intensity I've only seen a few times before—usually when he means business. Beside him is a slight woman with tight blonde hair, clutching a clipboard. She's familiar, but I can't place her. Must have seen her around the base.

"Sir," I reply crisply, drawing myself to attention. Whatever personal battle is raging inside me, I won't let it be visible to anyone else—least of all my superior.

Benedict steps inside and motions for the woman to follow. He doesn't waste any time, cutting straight to the point. No small talk, no meaningless pleasantries. It's not his style.

"Captain, I've heard some concerns," he says, his voice steady but tinged with something I can't quite identify. "Your wife came to see me."

My stomach tightens at the mention of Sierra. I should have expected this after our argument this morning, but hearing it from Benedict's mouth makes it all the more real. I clench my jaw, keeping my expression under control. I'm good at that. At least, I always used to be.

"She seems to think there's something ... different about you since the helo crash," he continues, watching me like a hawk. "She's worried. She thinks we should be, too."

I bite the inside of my cheek, searching for the right words. How do I explain to him what I barely understand myself?

Do I tell him about the inexplicable shifts in my memory, the sudden aversions, the feeling that I'm living someone else's life? And what if I'm wrong? What if this is just what happens when you spend too many years in the belly of the beast? The Marine Corps can do that to a man—pull him apart and stitch him back together with too many patches missing.

But Benedict is waiting for an explanation, and I have to give him something.

"With all due respect, sir," I start, measuring each word, "Sierra is understandably stressed. The crash and my recovery was ... difficult, but I've been cleared for duty. I'm fine."

Benedict doesn't seem convinced, but he's not pressing yet, just listening. He exchanges a glance with the blonde woman who jots something on her clipboard.

"I'm fine," I say again.

"I want you to expend some effort thinking things through. Consider what's really important."

I wince inwardly at that last line. The implication isn't lost on me. He isn't just talking about my commitment to the Corps.

"Yes, sir," I reply.

But the words taste bitter in my mouth. I've spent years honing my defenses, perfecting the mask of the unshakeable Marine. Lately, that mask feels like it's slipping. And Benedict, sharp as he is, can probably see the fractures.

He narrows his eyes, scrutinizing me in a way that makes

me feel like I'm under a microscope. "Look, Captain, I know what stress can do to a man. Psychological wounds can cut deeper than any shrapnel, bullet, or mangled wreckage. If there's anything you need to talk about, anything at all, you come to me. Don't let pride or protocol get in the way of your well-being. Understood?"

"Yes, sir," I respond, but my voice carries a hint of defensiveness. I don't need this. I just need everyone to get off my back, let me figure this out on my own.

He studies me for another moment, then nods, seemingly satisfied—for now. "All right. We're going to leave you to it, but remember what I said. Spend some time. Think it over."

Benedict turns to leave, but then something flickers across his expression—a hesitation, a thought that he hasn't yet decided to voice. He glances back, as if weighing whether to say more, but then brushes it off.

"Dismissed," he finally says, curtly.

The blonde assistant scribbles something final on her clipboard, then follows Benedict out, leaving me alone in the sterile room. The door clicks shut behind them, and the silence that follows is almost deafening.

I exhale, long and deep, trying to chain down the turmoil that's thrumming beneath my skin.

What the hell am I supposed to think about? I've already gone through my mental playbook a hundred times, reviewed every scenario, every possible explanation. Nothing makes sense.

I sit down heavily in the chair by the desk, running a hand through my short, dark hair. It feels like someone else's hair, someone else's head.

Sierra's words echo in my mind, clear and persistent. She sees the changes, the sleepless nights, but she can't see the full extent of what's happening inside. Can't see how each passing day makes me feel more like a shadow of myself, slipping further into some internal abyss.

Suddenly, the thought of going back to our house in Woodbridge, of lying in that same bed where every night becomes a wrestling match with a mind that no longer feels like my own, fills me with dread. How do you explain to someone that you don't even recognize the reflection staring back at you—not just in the mirror, but in your thoughts, in your actions, in the things that should make you, *you*?

I stand and walk over to the small window, staring out at the gray, overcast sky. There's no comfort in the weather, but it's better than the sterile walls of the room. For a moment, I wonder if there's any place on Earth that could feel comforting anymore.

I haven't been back to New York to visit my mother since the crash. I wonder if my childhood home would feel the same. Somehow, I doubt it.

The trees are barren, their branches skeletal against the backdrop of a steel-colored sky. More shadows than substance. That's how I feel—like a network of long, thin threads holding together a hollow form, one that's ready to snap in a stiff wind.

I can't keep this up much longer.

My mind drifts back to that helo crash—how everything spun out of control in the span of a few minutes. Before I can delve too deeply into my memories, though, the door behind me creaks as it opens. I turn, half-expecting to see Benedict again, or perhaps Sierra, demanding answers I still don't have.

But it's neither.

It's a man I've never met before. He stands in the doorway, backlit by the harsh fluorescent light of the hallway. He's tall, but not imposing—dressed in civilian clothes that somehow don't seem quite right for this place.

He steps into the room, the door clicking shut behind him, and the oppressive air thickens even more. He doesn't introduce himself, doesn't offer a handshake or any other kind of greeting. Instead, he studies me for a long moment, like he's examining a specimen.

"Captain Teague," he finally says, and there's no question in his tone. It's as if he's known me longer than I've known myself.

"Who are you?" I ask, but my voice, usually assertive, wavers slightly. There's an odd familiarity to him—a nagging sense that I should recognize him, but my mind draws a blank.

He chuckles softly, a sound devoid of humor, like he's amused by an inside joke I'm not privy to. "You don't remember, do you?"

The question sends a chill down my spine. There's something in the way he says it—like he's probing, testing the edges of a memory that doesn't belong to me.

"I asked who you are," I repeat, my tone hardening, but the slight tremor in my hand as I clench it into a fist betrays my unease.

He ignores the question, taking a slow, deliberate step towards me. "Catherine was right," he murmurs, more to himself than to me. "We might've pushed too far."

I freeze at the name, feeling like I've been struck. Catherine? The name doesn't belong to anyone I know—at least, not that I can recall.

Before I can ask him what he means, he tilts his head, as if studying an intricate puzzle. "Tell me, Captain, how often do you sleep?"

I blink, caught off guard. "That's none of your business."

He arches an eyebrow. "Humor me."

I don't answer, and his expression shifts slightly. There's something in his eyes that unnerves me—a sharpness, an intelligence that sees straight through me to the core I've been so desperately trying to protect.

"You don't, do you?" he presses. "Not really. Not since the crash."

The words hit harder than I care to admit. "Who the hell are you?" I demand, taking a step forward. My pulse quickens, though I keep my expression as neutral as possible. I'm aware of the door behind him, of the distance between us. Every tactical detail has become suddenly sharp in my mind, clouded by a tight knot of fear I refuse to let rise past the surface.

"My name isn't important." He pauses, weighing his words carefully. "But what I represent ... that's another story."

I don't know why, but my breath catches. My instincts tell me this man represents more than just himself. He's here for a reason, and I've got the cold, sinking feeling that reason has everything to do with the gnawing empty feeling I've been battling since that crash.

He steps closer, eyes locking onto mine with a predatory intensity. "We've been watching you, Captain Teague. You're valuable ... you can be useful to us. But only if you remember."

"Remember what?" I snap, frustration and confusion boiling over. My hand twitches towards the knife sheathed at my side before I catch myself. Fight or flight instincts flare up, but I force them back down. This is a situation that demands control, not violence. Not yet.

He studies me for another moment before a faint, inscrutable smile tugs at the corner of his lips. "Who you really are. Who they made you to be."

Something in the way he says *they* sends a chill through my bones. I want to press him, demand answers, but the words catch in my throat.

He turns away slightly, pacing in a slow circle as if contemplating how much to reveal. "It's not about the crash, Captain. That was just ... a catalyst. The real changes? They started much earlier. You had potential, but we needed to test your limits. To see what would happen when we introduced ... certain variables."

My head starts to throb, a dull ache spreading across my temples. "What variables? What the hell are you talking about?"

He stops, turning back to face me with eyes that now seem almost too sharp, too knowing. "You're not just Captain Teague. The man you think you are, the life you think you've lived—it's been constructed, manipulated. You're something more, something different. And it's time you started embracing that difference."

The pounding in my head intensifies, a terrible pressure building as flashes of unrecognizable faces and places start to push forward. But nothing sticks. It's like trying to grasp smoke with bare hands—close, too close, but always just out of reach.

"I don't believe you," I say, though the conviction in my voice falters. If he's lying, why does everything in me feel like it's screaming that he's right?

"You will," he says, almost sympathetically. "When you're ready, you'll understand why things are different now. And then, you'll have a choice to make."

Chapter Three

SIERRA

"You're so lucky," Beth Tucker says as she admires my wedding rings. Her curly blonde hair dances around her shoulders as she moves.

Beth was out of the country, studying abroad, when Oscar and I got married last year. This is the first time my best friend has seen my rings. It's the first time she'll meet my husband, too. He'll be home from work in a few hours, and the three of us are going to dinner at Luigi's Italian Kitchen on the Chesapeake Bay.

"Yeah, I suppose I am," I reply, trying hard to keep my smile from falling.

The rings glitter beneath the dim light of our kitchen, throwing tiny rainbows across the granite countertop. I should feel proud showing them off to Beth, should feel happy that she's finally here, sharing this part of my life. But the truth is, those rings are starting to feel heavier every day, like chains rather than symbols of love.

"Suppose?" Beth shoots me a skeptical glance, setting

down her cup of coffee. Her polished nails shine. “Sierra, this is a rock! And Oscar sounds practically perfect. You should be over the moon, my friend.”

I force a laugh, a sound that sticks in my throat. “Yeah, I know. It’s just ... married life’s been a little more complicated than I imagined.”

Beth’s perfectly-manicured eyebrows knit together in concern. “Complicated? How so?”

I hesitate, trying to find the right words. How do you explain that the man Beth has heard me talk about for so long, the man she’s about to meet, is barely recognizable to me anymore? That the husband she’s so eager to meet is a stranger cloaked in Oscar’s familiar skin?

“He’s changed,” I reply finally, keeping it vague. “You know, work stress, the helicopter crash ... It’s been tough on him.”

Beth nods, her expression softening with understanding. “I get it. Dad still isn’t the same after that car accident. New jobs, new stress—sometimes it’s hard for people to adjust.”

I nod appreciatively, though her words, however well-meaning, don’t come close to the storm brewing inside me.

This is different. This isn’t just stress or readjusting after trauma. I hate to say it, but I think this is something deeper, darker—something I can’t quite place but terrifies me all the same.

“You’re right,” I agree. “There’s always been a tension there, though. Oscar has never been at ease quite like ...”

Sensing my hesitation, Beth reaches across the table and squeezes my hand. Her charm bracelet jangles cheerfully, even though I'm not in a cheerful mood. “You can say his name,” she says softly.

She knows exactly who I'm referring to.

"Norm."

Norman Chaben was my boyfriend in college who died in a mountain climbing accident. We'd been deeply in love, and I assumed I'd marry him one day. Those plans changed when his life was cut tragically short, of course. Norman was the epitome of easy going. He had a sense of peace about him like no one else I've ever known. His first words were probably the lyrics to "Kumbaya." That or "Let It Be."

I love Oscar dearly, but there's always been an edge to him. An edge Norm didn't have. That edge has just sharpened. I fear it will only continue to sharpen.

Oh, well. What does it matter about Norm, at this point? I love the man I married. No use thinking about what might have been.

"Hey, if there's anything I can do," Beth says with an understanding smile, "just let me know, okay? I'm here for you."

A rush of gratitude floods through me, though it's tinged with sadness. I don't want to burden Beth with my fears—not now, not when she's just come back into my life. Add her study-abroad time to grad school, and it's been years since we've lived in the same city. So, I muster the most genuine smile I can and squeeze her hand back.

"Thanks, Beth. I appreciate that. I really do."

The doorbell rings, breaking the moment, and my stomach twists with a mix of anticipation and dread. "That must be Oscar," I say, trying to keep my voice light, but the tightness in my chest tells an entirely different story.

How did this become my life?

Beth beams, clearly excited to finally meet the man I used

to gush about during our late-night phone calls. I don't have the heart to tell her that the person standing on the other side of the door might not be the Oscar she's expecting.

I force myself to stand and walk towards the door, each step more difficult than the last. My hand trembles slightly as I reach for the doorknob, the cool metal grounding me. Though it offers little solace as I twist it and pull the door open.

There he is. Or at least, there's someone who looks like him.

Oscar stands in the doorway, his presence dominating the space, but there's something different—something subtly unsettling—that I can't put my finger on. It's shifted even since this morning. He's dressed casually, in jeans and a dark sweater, his stance relaxed. He looks as handsome as ever. But his eyes, once warm and inviting, now hold a cold, distant gleam.

"Hey," he says, his voice familiar but lacking the warmth I used to find so comforting. He leans down to kiss me on the cheek, but the gesture feels mechanical, forced. Like something he knows he's supposed to do but no longer understands why.

"Hey, yourself," I reply, hoping he can't hear the tremor in my voice.

Oscar steps inside, and when he does, his gaze flickers to Beth. It's only for a fraction of a second, but it's enough. I see it in his eyes—a flash of something unreadable, something that shouldn't be there.

"Oscar, this is Beth, my best friend from college. As you know, she was studying abroad when we got married, so ..." I trail off, unsure of where I'm going with this.

Oscar smiles, but it doesn't reach his eyes. "Nice to finally meet you," he says, extending his hand toward Beth.

Beth takes it eagerly, her face lighting up. "It's great to meet you, too, Oscar. Sierra's told me so much about you."

Oscar's smile becomes a little wider, but there's still something off, something distant in the way he interacts with her. It's like he's playing a role. One he's not entirely comfortable with.

"Yeah, she's mentioned you often as well," Oscar replies, his tone practiced. Smooth.

I'm not sure if Beth notices. She's locked into the moment, likely soaking up this long-awaited introduction. It's only been a few minutes, but I'm already watching Beth and Oscar with the careful eye of a clinical observer rather than a wife reuniting with her husband and her best friend.

Beth hasn't seen him in person before. To her, Oscar is still the man from the stories I've spun over countless late-night wine-fueled calls, the same ones where I gushed about how he made me feel safe and adored.

But that was before. Before the "helo crash," as I've grown used to calling it. Before the world shifted, before Oscar turned into this facsimile of himself—familiar in appearance, but deeply wrong at the core. A strange dread gnaws at me as I watch him interact with Beth, as if he's trying on emotions he's lost, attempting to mimic them convincingly enough to hide the cracks in his mask.

"So, how was the return trip home to the States?" he asks Beth, his voice a little too precise, every syllable measured out in doses like a drug to induce calm.

"Oh, long but uneventful, which is all you can ask for

when you're stuck on a seventeen-hour journey," Beth says with a laugh.

Her charm never fails. She has a way of diffusing tension, and right now it's like a bright warmth against the growing shadow I feel in the room. "It feels good to be back. I've missed the good ol' U. S. of A., and I've missed Sierra like crazy." She turns her brilliant smile back on me.

But when Oscar's smile doesn't waver, that chill that's been growing inside me turns into solid ice.

I don't know what I'm expecting. He stays static, perfectly composed, like a soldier in formation, waiting for the moment the mask can drop again. He doesn't feel anymore—I'm becoming sure of it—and it has something to do with what happened that day he fell from the sky.

Oscar shifts his weight forward, the gesture casual but there's a curious lack of energy. "I'm sure it's been great catching up. Ready for dinner?"

His words cut through whatever lingering merriment there is, catching us off guard. He doesn't wait for an answer before he's turning toward the door, pulling the keys from his pocket.

"Luigi's?" he says as he glances back at me, his tone still pleasant, still surface-level. It's like he's reading from a script —an automaton programmed to carry out the scene without any real engagement.

"Y-Yeah," I respond, a tremor in my voice that I hope Beth doesn't notice.

Who am I kidding? I know she's perceptive. She must be catching on, even if she doesn't fully understand. I can see the slight furrow in her brow, the way her smile falters for the briefest moment before she recovers.

"Great! Can't wait to dig into some real American pasta," Beth jokes, trying to rekindle the lightness.

She's good at that.

Oscar nods, the smile still in place, but I can tell it's a mask, a thin layer of camouflage barely concealing whatever is lurking beneath.

I grab my coat from the rack by the door, and Beth does the same. As we make our way outside, I glance back at Oscar, who's already out the door ahead of us, walking toward the car with a purpose that feels slightly off. He moves just a beat too fast, like he's eager to get this over with.

The sky above is descending quickly into evening, the air crisp and biting as we step into the chilly breeze. The gray overcast from the afternoon has deepened, as if setting the stage for the creeping sense of foreboding that's been gnawing at me all day.

Isn't it twisted? That I'm more nervous about how Oscar will behave tonight than about his safety in a war zone? That I've become so absorbed in hiding the hollowness I feel that even having Beth here feels like I'm putting on a show—one where the heroine is hopelessly trying to convince the world, and herself, that everything is fine. When really, the spotlight has turned cold, the lead actor has shifted, and the play has taken an unsettling turn.

I open the passenger door and slide in while Oscar starts the car. Beth takes her place in the backseat, chatting away in her usual animated style, trying to draw us both into conversation. She asks about the house, about Quantico, and about our plans for the spring.

Oscar humors her, as best as he can, answering her questions with the same rehearsed ease that has become alarmingly familiar. His voice is steady, his responses polite, but there's no passion behind them. No true engagement.

Beth, however, is undeterred. She presses on, asking about the local sights, military life, anything to keep the conversation alive, and I can't help but admire her effort, even as I silently scream for the car ride to be over.

As we drive toward Luigi's, the tension in the car grows. None of us acknowledge it, but it's there—settling into every word, every pause, every lingering look. I keep my eyes fixed out the window, watching as the trees blur into dark forms against the encroaching dusk.

Is this my life now? Tiptoeing around my husband, pretending that everything is normal while secretly wondering if the man beside me is even the same person I fell in love with?

I hope things get better. I truly do.

When we finally arrive at Luigi's, I exhale with relief, eager to get out of the car and away from the suffocating atmosphere inside it. Oscar parks the car with precision, the motion smooth but almost too calculated, like he's completing a task assigned to him rather than simply parking a car.

We step out into the cool evening air, and I wrap my coat tighter around my body, grounding myself in the sensation of the fabric against my skin. Beth chatters beside me, her voice the only warm note amidst the gray elements.

Oscar is ahead of us, his pace brisk as he leads the way to the restaurant entrance.

Luigi's is a cozy place, a favorite of the local community, where the scent of garlic and fresh basil greets you as soon as you step through the door. The warm, amber lighting and rustic décor give it a comforting ambiance, which I desperately need right now. Maybe if I can focus on the simple pleasures—some good wine, a comforting meal, the company of my best friend—I can make it through this evening without letting the icy dread in my veins take over.

We're seated at a small table near the window, where the faint glow of street lamps filters through the glass, casting a soft light over our faces. Beth immediately comments on how adorable the place is, and I find myself nodding automatically, trying to latch onto something, anything, that might make this night feel like a slice of normal life.

"Good choice, Sierra," she says. "If the food tastes anything like it smells, we're all in for a treat."

Oscar takes his seat across from me, folding the napkin on his lap with an elegance that seems far removed from the man I fell in love with—the fun-loving, charismatic Marine who always had a grin on his face and a light in his eyes that made me feel like the world was still a wonderful place.

Now, that light is gone, replaced by a steely coldness that feels almost ... calculated.

He begins scanning the menu with a laser-sharp focus, as if every item holds some deep secret he must unlock. It's unsettling—this hyper-focused attention to menial tasks while completely avoiding the emotional landscape between us.

As we place our orders, I try to engage him in conversation. Raising my voice just a little, I say, "Oscar, do you remember that time we went to that tiny Italian place in Naples on our honeymoon? The one where they had all those crazy flavors of gelato?"

I watch him carefully for any reaction, hoping to see a

flicker of recognition in his eyes—a shared memory that might soften the strain between us. But Oscar's gaze remains distant, as if the weight of my words barely registers.

"Yeah," he says after a slight pause, "the gelato was decent."

Beth looks between us, no doubt sensing the underlying tension, and quickly tries to bring some levity. "Oh, I remember you telling me about that place! You said Oscar was a total gelato aficionado. He tried the weirdest flavors, right?"

I force a smile, grateful for her attempt, but the words feel hollow. The man before me isn't the one who dove headfirst into an obscure flavor of gelato without hesitation, grinning like a kid as he dared me to try it, too.

This Oscar barely seems to care.

"Yeah, he did," I reply, though the cheerful tone comes out more muted than I intended. "Salted caramel and olive oil. Not exactly a classic combo, but he loved it."

Oscar looks up, locking eyes with me, and I can't help but notice how empty his gaze seems, like he's dredging up a memory he should have, but it lacks any real color. Just an outline of a picture he's trying to recall from hearsay rather than experience.

"It was an interesting flavor," Oscar says, offering a bleak imitation of the grin that should accompany such a memory. But it doesn't reach his eyes. There's no warmth in the expression—just a mechanical, almost robotic acknowledgment of the past.

Iit shatters something inside me.

His words are there, but the person isn't. The one who relished taking risks in life, even when it came to something as simple as a gelato flavor, has been replaced by this ... stranger.

Beth, ever the optimist, presses on. "Sounds like you two had quite the adventure together." Her tone is light, but I can feel the underlying concern seeping through her words. She's starting to sense something is very, very wrong.

"Yeah," I murmur, my gaze fixed on Oscar. "It was amazing."

Beth picks up on my hesitation, her smile faltering slightly before she quickly regains her usual positivity. "You know what? We should plan another adventure," she suggests, her voice brightening the mood just a little. "The three of us. How about a road trip to the Outer Banks? I hear the beaches are gorgeous, and I've always wanted to see some of the wild mustangs there."

Oscar's eyes flick towards her, and for a moment, I think he's going to refuse—dismiss the idea with one of those cold, calculated responses that have become his default lately. But then, in a move that surprises me, he nods, though there's no enthusiasm in the motion.

"Yeah, that could be nice," he says, his words perfectly composed, devoid of the playfulness he used to have when we'd plan spontaneous trips.

Beth beams, seemingly satisfied with this tiny victory, and yet I can't shake the growing pit in my stomach. The man sitting across from me might share Oscar's face, his voice, and some of his mannerisms, but underneath it all, he's someone I don't recognize.

The waiter arrives, taking our orders with the efficient politeness characteristic of little family-owned places like Luigi's. Once he's gone, I turn my attention back to the two people seated with me. Oscar has resumed his meticulous study of the menu, though he's already told the waiter what he wanted.

Beth flashes me a look, one of those silent, concerned glances that best friends exchange when they know something's wrong but aren't sure how to bring it up.

Chapter Four

OSCAR

“Actually, I don’t want to make any plans,” I say instinctively, too quickly. My voice cuts through the remaining small talk between Sierra and Beth like a knife, and the atmosphere at our cozy table grows suddenly taut.

I see Sierra flinch ever so slightly, her dark eyes widening in that way I’ve come to recognize as her being hurt but trying to hide it.

I don't wish to hurt my wife.

My words hang in the air, and I feel an unfamiliar pang of guilt twist in my chest. It’s not that I don’t want to spend time with her. It’s that the thought of pretending, of wearing this mask of normalcy any longer, is suffocating.

Beth raises an eyebrow, her cheerful expression faltering briefly. “Oh, come on, Oscar. Road trips are fun! It’ll be a chance for us to all relax and enjoy some downtime.”

She’s trying. I can see that. Trying to bring back some semblance of light to this oppressive evening, but I’m just not capable of engaging in it. My mind doesn’t even compute the concept of fun right now. Everything feels detached, numb, as though I'm interacting with the world through a thick pane of glass.

"I'm ... sorry, Beth," I add, realizing too late how cold I sounded. It's strange, the words feel like they're coming from someone else's mouth. "I'm just dealing with a lot at work right now. Maybe some other time ... when things settle down."

It's a lie, the usual polite dismissal I've gotten too good at using lately. General Benedict's words earlier today flicker in my mind. He told me to consider what's really important. I should be trying harder to connect, to rebuild whatever's been dismantled since the crash. Instead, I feel the walls around my mind closing tighter, resisting any attempt to break them down.

"No worries," Beth says, still smiling, but her eyes—sharp and perceptive like Sierra's—are studying me too intently. "I get it. We all have our moments."

I nod, offering a tight-lipped smile in return. There's no warmth in it, I know that, but I can't fake what I don't feel.

As the conversation limps along, I find myself barely able to keep track of what's being said. My focus drifts as if carried away by an unseen current, sweeping me into murkier waters where nothing seems clear or certain.

The memory of that strange man from earlier today, the one who somehow knew more about me than he had any right to, claws its way to the forefront of my mind. His cryptic comments replay in a continuous loop. What did he mean that I'm not the man I think I am? I try to piece together fragments.

A hollow feeling spreads through my chest, and I rub at it

absently, hoping the physical action might dispel the discomfort.

Did I always rub my chest this way? I think so. But maybe not.

Sierra's voice breaks through the haze, bringing me back to the present. "Oscar? Are you okay?"

She's looking at me with an expression of concern that nearly breaks me. It's the same look she's been giving me more and more—a mixture of worry, fear, and something approaching desperation. She wants to help. I know she genuinely does.

How can she, when I don't even know what's wrong?

I nod, forcing another strained smile to my face. "Yeah, I'm fine, just a bit tired. Long day."

I can tell she doesn't entirely believe me, but she offers me an out by turning the conversation back to Beth. Part of me is grateful for the reprieve, but another part screams at me to reach out, to tell Sierra everything, no matter how nonsensical it sounds.

How do you explain something that feels so irrational? I can't exactly say, "Hey, honey, by the way, I think I might not actually be the man you married. Also, I've been having some weird, ominous conversations with strangers. Maybe I'm having some sort of mental breakdown."

Yeah, that would definitely go over well. I can already hear the pity in her voice, the uncertainty in her eyes.

The plates arrive at our table, steaming with the inviting aroma of garlic, basil, and tomatoes, but the food might as well be cardboard for all the appetite I have. I go through the motions, cutting into my pasta and chicken parmesan, taking a few bites, nodding along as Beth and Sierra talk, but everything is mechanical.

There's a part of me that recognizes the taste and recalls the pleasure this dish used to give me. My mother used to make it for me when I was a kid in New York. Only these flavors are dull, the textures foreign. I wonder if I'd feel the same about my mother's cooking now. I wonder if I'll ever enjoy food again.

Are my tastebuds somehow irreparably damaged?

"Tastes good," I say, for no particular reason.

Beth is laughing at something Sierra said—a joke I didn't catch. She glances at me, probably expecting me to share in the laughter, to smile or at least acknowledge that I'm part of this moment. I force the corners of my mouth up, but it feels like a lie. A hollow, lifeless lie.

I can see Sierra out of the corner of my eye, studying me when she thinks I'm not looking. She's always watching, always worried, like she's waiting for something to crack or fall apart. And who knows, maybe she's right? Maybe something inside me is already in pieces, scattered and lost.

I have no idea how to put it back together.

"Remember the time we got lost trying to find Cadillac Ranch?" Sierra says, turning to me, her voice filled with forced cheer. "Beth, you should've seen it. Oscar insisted we didn't need a GPS, and we ended up driving two hours in the wrong direction. But he was so determined to make it to that place, we laughed about it the whole way back."

I muster a chuckle, trying to summon the memory, but it's hazy, indistinct—like a fragment of a dream that vanishes as soon as you wake up. I remember the road trip vaguely, the oppressive Texas heat, the endless miles of flat, barren land. But the laughter? The joy? Those are difficult to recall.

"Yeah," I say, nodding along like I do remember, but there's no conviction in my voice, no substance behind the words.

Sierra's expression falters—the brightness in her eyes dimming just enough for me to notice. The sparkle that once made her eyes light up at the mention of a shared memory is gone, replaced by a flicker of something more sorrowful.

I know she's trying, grasping onto these past moments, hoping they'll break through whatever wall has formed between us. But it's like reaching into the dark, hoping to find a light that just isn't there anymore.

Beth seems to catch the shift in the atmosphere between us as well. Her gaze shifts from Sierra to me and back again, the humor fading from her face. She clears her throat, clearly uncomfortable with the tension. She's too polite to address it outright.

I pick up my fork and push the pasta around on my plate. It's like I'm playing the role of "Oscar," the husband, the Marine, the person these two women expect me to be. Inside, I feel nothing but a slow, growing emptiness.

How much longer can I keep this up?

The more I try to grasp at the fragments of the life I've known, the more they slip through my fingers, leaving me with this cold, numb detachment that I can't shake. The man who fell in love with Sierra, who made her laugh and held her close on those lazy Sunday mornings—that man feels like a ghost. A distant memory.

All I want is to find him again. But how?

Beth tries to fill the silence, reaching for another thread of conversation.

"You know, I met this amazing street artist in Paris," she says. "He had this way of capturing all the vibrant colors of the city. It was almost like he was painting a piece of its soul..." she trails off when she sees that neither of us are really engaged.

I glance at Sierra, seeing the way she picks at her food, her gaze cast down at the table. It's as if I've been handed a tiny glimpse into her inner turmoil, and it's a mirror of my own. I should reach out. Say something that will bridge the gulf between us. Unfortunately, the words won't come. Instead, I feel myself slipping further into the abyss, where reaching out seems impossible.

"Seems like Sierra and I are both tired tonight," I try feebly.

The three of us finish our meals in near silence. It's only Beth's attempts at small talk that ripple through it, and only superficially. She tells us about her trips and recent adventures, but her enthusiasm only serves to highlight the lack of it in the people she's talking to.

The check comes, and I pull out my wallet automatically, insistently taking care of the bill before the ladies can protest. Even that feels practiced, just another part of the performance. It's what a good Marine should do.

An officer and a gentleman, right?

As we slip out of the restaurant into the cool evening air, I stare up at the sky. The stars are out, their faint glimmer barely piercing through the light pollution from the city. They seem distant, barely connected to the world I'm walking through—much like how I feel in this moment.

Beth stretches her arms above her head, yawning slightly as she turns towards us with a half-smile.

"Well, that was delicious," she says. "Thanks for dinner, Oscar. It's really great to finally hang out with you both."

Her words are cheerful, but I can sense the undercurrent of concern in her tone. She has questions she hasn't dared ask, doubts that she's keeping locked away out of respect for Sierra. I wonder how long it will be until she finally confronts them—or me—directly. It's only a matter of time.

Sierra forces a smile, nodding in agreement with Beth's sentiment. "Yeah ... it was nice. We should do it again sometime."

There's a half-heartedness in her voice that she can't hide, and it cuts deeper than I care to admit. This erosion of who I once was has taken a toll on us both, and we've been reduced to fumbling through the remnants of a relationship that once was solid.

Beth's gaze lingers on me for a beat too long before she pulls out her phone to check the time. "I should get going. I have an early day tomorrow. I'll call for a car. But thanks again for dinner. It was really great seeing you, Sierra."

She turns to me, her look soft and understanding. "And you too, Oscar. I hope ... things get better."

It's the most benign, non-specific way of acknowledging the elephant in the room. She's too polite to demand answers now, but like Sierra, Beth is perceptive, and I can feel her concern.

"Thanks, Beth," I reply, my tone as neutral as ever. I manage another hollow smile. "Be safe getting home."

She's living in D.C. now, so I suspect I'll be seeing more of her.

Sierra and Beth exchange a quick hug, and then Beth turns, heading off in the opposite direction. I watch her walk away, feeling as though a piece of normalcy has slipped through my grasp again.

As Beth's silhouette fades in the distance, the silence between Sierra and me grows even more pronounced. The tension that had been momentarily dampened by the distraction of Beth's presence now returns with full force, wrapping around us like the bitter evening cold.

Chapter Five

SIERRA

As Beth disappears into the night, the chill returns, heavier than before.

Oscar's silence next to me feels oppressive, as if something unsaid is choking the air between us. For a moment, I consider letting it go, burying whatever I've been feeling deep inside, just to preserve the fragile peace we've managed to maintain this evening.

We stand there, lingering outside the restaurant as though waiting for the night to offer us some sort of absolution. The words hang heavy on the tip of my tongue, begging to be released, but I hesitate. I don't want to confront this here, in this cold, exposed place. Yet the need for answers is gnawing at me too fiercely to ignore.

Oscar stares blankly at the darkened horizon, his gaze distant, almost as if he's contemplating an exit from this world altogether. It only solidifies my resolve—whatever's happening to him cannot continue to go unspoken between us any longer.

"Oscar," I begin tentatively, "Can we talk? And I don't

mean just conversation filler—but really talk? I feel like I don't know who you are anymore, and it scares the hell out of me."

My voice trembles but steadies as I press forward, my heart hammering against my ribs.

I've tried to remain patient, to offer him the space I thought he might need. That patience is fraying. I'm at my breaking point.

Oscar doesn't look at me right away. He remains still, jaw tight, eyes locked on something unseen in the distance. Then slowly, wordlessly, he nods.

"Okay," he says quietly, his voice low and devoid of any real emotion. His agreement feels like a mere formality rather than a willing engagement, but it's something, and I latch onto it.

"Let's not do this here," I say, shivering slightly from the cold and from the tension boiling beneath the surface. "Let's go home."

Oscar finally moves, turning towards me, and there's something in his eyes—some fleeting emotion that I can't quite decipher. Is it regret? Resignation? Despair? I'm not sure, but it feels like he might be on the verge of telling me something.

As I look at him, I can't help but think about how deeply I love this man. We had a grand love. One for the ages. It was everything I'd ever dreamed of. What's happening between us breaks my heart.

The drive back home is a blurry haze of thoughts and silence. Oscar doesn't say a word the entire ride, his hands gripping the wheel with a kind of restrained tension that makes me wonder if he's holding himself together with sheer willpower alone. I glance over at him occasionally, hoping for some sign—anything—that might give me insight into what's brewing inside him. But all I see is the muscle in his jaw ticking, a small, involuntary motion that betrays the tempest beneath his otherwise emotionless exterior.

The trees along the road stretch like skeletal arms, reaching out to the vehicle as we pass, the moon casting eerie silver highlights onto the twisted branches. It feels like the landscape itself mirrors my inner turmoil—something cold and lifeless, stripped of all warmth and vitality. I wonder when it happened, when everything that made us "us" started to dissolve like this.

Did the Marine Corps do it to him? Does this happen to other high-ranking officers? I suddenly wish I'd taken classes on military psychology. My clinical training at Emory had only mentioned it as an afterthought. There's so much to cover in the field, and specialization is key. I'm a child psychologist. As such, the focus of my training was on child and adolescent development.

I'm at a loss, in more ways than one.

When my husband finally pulls into the driveway, the house looms before us. The place that once felt like a sanctuary is now overshadowed by darkness and dread. He cuts the engine but makes no move to get out, the silence stretching unbearably within the confines of the car.

I can't stand it anymore.

"Oscar," I say, breaking the silence that's grown a little too comfortable even in its discomfort. "Please ... just talk to me. I need to understand what's happening to us. To you."

He turns to me, and for a moment, I think I see a flash of something in his eyes—fear, maybe, or guilt—but it's gone almost as quickly as it appeared. All that's left is the cold steel of his resolve.

"I don't know what you want me to say," he admits, and his voice drips with exhaustion. "I ... I don't have answers. Hell, Sierra, I don't even know who I am right now."

His words are like a knife twisting in my gut, confirming the fears that I've tried so hard to suppress. He's lost—detached from himself, from *us*—and no amount of pretending seems able to bridge the abyss that's opened between us.

"I feel like I'm losing you," I whisper, my voice cracking under the weight of the admission. "And I don't know how to stop it."

It's out there now. The raw, vulnerable truth I've been too afraid to speak. Tears prick at my eyes, and I bite my lip, refusing to let the floodgates open. I'm tired—*so* tired—of holding it all in. Of pretending that I'm okay when I'm anything but.

Oscar looks away, his jaw clenched so tightly that I can see the muscles straining.

"I don't want to lose you, Sierra," he says, his voice barely above a whisper. "But I don't know how to find myself. I feel ... fragmented, like I'm walking around in a skin that doesn't fit anymore."

He pauses for a long time on the word *fragmented*.

His confession feels like a lifeline, something real and raw, even as despair claws its way deeper into my heart.

"Then let me help you," I plead, reaching out to grab his hand. "Whatever it is ... we can face it together. You don't have to go through this alone."

He looks down at our hands—mine wrapped tightly

around his, desperate to ground him and, perhaps, ground myself too. But that same detachment in his eyes flickers, and I know I'm fighting a losing battle with something I can't even fully comprehend.

"I don't know if this is something you can help with," he admits, a note of resignation tainting his words. "Sometimes, I'm scared that if you knew ... if you really understood what's going on inside my head, you wouldn't recognize me anymore. Maybe you'd leave."

His words slice through me with the cruelty of an icy wind. The man I love is broken, but he's also scared. Scared that his darkness, whatever it is, will consume the most precious thing in his life.

"I'm not going anywhere, Oscar," I say, with as much conviction as I can muster. "I married you for better or worse. I just need you to let me in. Please."

He nods, but it's a hollow movement, void of any real commitment. "Let's go inside," he finally says, pulling his hand away from mine gently but firmly. "This conversation is not an easy one, and it's too cold to be having it out here."

We slip out of the car, and I follow him up the steps to the front door. The house, still and silent, greets us with the kind of quiet that feels ominous instead of comforting.

Oscar inserts the key into the lock, and as we step inside, I realize that the warmth of our home isn't enough to dispel the chill that seems to have settled into my bones. The momentary warmth of the heater kicking on greets us, but it feels out of place—like a ghost of the home we once shared, now filled with shadows I can't quite grasp.

Oscar doesn't turn on the lights. He guides us through the darkened rooms with the confidence of someone who knows his way but avoids any sense of familiarity. His steps are measured, precise, as if he's on autopilot, leading us towards the living room without acknowledging the seriousness of the conversation we are about to have.

The curtain is still drawn back. If someone outside wanted to look in, they could. Our nosy neighbor, Ms. Brattenbah, might like to do exactly that.

We sit down on opposite ends of the couch, a wide chasm between us both physically and emotionally. I pull a throw blanket over my lap. My hands fidget with the blue fringe, twisting it in nervous knots as I wait for him to start. He leans back, his elbows resting on his knees, head bowed as if gathering his thoughts.

I can imagine him in this stance at his job. He probably gets into this exact position when briefing his subordinates on a mission. I know his work is intense. I don't mean to ever make light of what he does for a living. The pressure changes people, I know that much for sure. Oscar's accident only served to amplify the nasty effects of a career where warfare is a primary focus.

Finally, he looks up, but the man staring back at me is still guarded, veiled in an impenetrable wall of grief, fear, and something darker—something I can't quite name.

"I've been having these ... episodes," he starts, his voice barely above a murmur. "Things I can't explain, like ... memory lapses, but they're more than that. It's like pieces of my life are missing, or worse—replaced by something foreign."

Cold ripples of fear wash over me, and I can barely keep my voice steady. I already knew, but hearing him say it out loud makes it real.

"What do you mean, replaced? Like someone else's memories?" I ask.

He winces, as if the words themselves cause him pain, and he nods slowly. "Maybe. Or dreams that feel real, but they're not dreams—they're memories of things I shouldn't have the faintest clue about, Sierra."

I grasp the edges of the blanket tighter around me, my heart sinking further as his words start to echo all the things I haven't wanted to acknowledge. Oscar isn't just struggling—he's unraveling at the seams. It sounds like he's delusional. Perhaps even hallucinating.

"And then there's the detachment," he continues, his voice strained as if each confession costs him dearly. "It's like I'm viewing everything about my life from a distance. Even how I feel about you. I know I care, I know I want to be the man you married, but it's getting harder every day to connect with those emotions."

I can't help the tears brimming in my eyes now. This pain, raw and unfiltered, is so much more than I ever anticipated. It's not just that Oscar's changed—he's becoming someone else, someone even he doesn't understand. The fear of losing him to this unknowable force twists in my gut, but so does the relentless hope that somehow, some way, I can save him. Save us.

"Oscar, have you thought about seeing a psychologist? Maybe there's—"

He cuts me off, shaking his head with something nearing frustration. "That's the problem, Sierra. I don't know if therapy will help. Hell, I don't even know if it's just in my head." His voice drops to a whisper, and I watch as a shadow seems to flicker across his face. "What if this is something else? Something they did to me?"

His words send a jolt through me, cold and sharp. *They?*

"Who?" I ask, though my voice barely makes it out.

He leans back again, rubbing his face with both hands as though trying to wipe away the thoughts that torment him.

"I don't know. I've had these flashes, moments of clarity, where I remember pieces of something ... like someone else's plan, like I was part of something bigger. But it doesn't make any sense, and it terrifies me. And then the memories slip away, leaving this emptiness, like a void that's sucking me in. And these ... these people I think I've seen—they're real, but they're not right. They're not supposed to be in my life."

My mind races, tumbling through every possibility, but none of it fits or makes sense. Whatever this is, I'm beginning to believe it's far beyond the stress of his military career. It's something darker, more insidious, clawing at the foundation of everything we once knew.

"Oscar," I say, inching closer to him, forcing him to meet my gaze. "We need help, real help. Maybe not just a psychologist. What about a neurologist? Could it have something to do with the crash? Brain trauma can do strange things. Impulse changes, memory problems ..."

I trail off, searching his expression for any sign of agreement.

He remains silent for a moment, eyes downcast, as though weighing my words on some invisible scale. Then slowly, he nods, but it's a small nod, one that speaks more to hopelessness.

What are we going to do?

Chapter Six

OSCAR

"No fucking doctors. No fucking tests."

The words leave my mouth before I have a chance to think about them, a harsh command rather than a suggestion. I can see the hurt and confusion flash across Sierra's face, but I can't take it back. I won't.

She doesn't understand. How could she?

The idea of doctors probing, analyzing, and digging into my brain like it's some kind of puzzle to be solved sends a wave of panic crashing through me. I've spent years giving everything to the Marine Corps, enduring endless physicals, psychological evaluations, training regimens, you name it. All under the guise of making me stronger, more resilient, and more effective.

But now? Now, I don't trust them. Or anyone.

What if they find something? What if they see what's happening in my head and decide I'm no longer fit to serve? Or worse? What if they've already done something to me, and they're waiting for it to play out? The man earlier today—whoever the hell he was—insinuated that there's more to this than I understand, more than I might ever know. But there are no concrete answers, only questions. And the fragments of memories that flit in and out of my mind feel more like traps than clues.

There's no solace in finding out I might be right.

Oscar, you need help. I hear Sierra's words echo in my mind, the plea in her voice.

No help can erase this. No shrink or neurologist can piece together something that has been—maybe intentionally—disassembled.

Sierra's hand settles gently on my knee, offering comfort, though I can sense her frustration simmering beneath the surface. "You can't just ignore this. We can't ignore this."

"I'm not ignoring it," I say, but the bitterness in my tone makes it clear that I'm pushing something down, something threatening to spill over. "I just—there are things I need to figure out on my own. Going to a doctor isn't going to give us answers. It might make everything worse."

"Worse?" she asks, her eyes searching mine, looking for some level of understanding I can't seem to reach. "How could it get worse? Oscar, you're falling apart. We're falling apart."

Her voice trembles on the edge of breaking, and that's when I feel it—the tight squeeze in my chest, the guilt bearing down on me like a physical weight.

"I know," I admit, my voice raw.

The confession seems to hang in the air between us. I've been trying to deny it, to downplay the truth, but there's no way I can cover it up anymore. We're standing on the brink of losing everything that once made sense. Everything that once mattered.

Sierra's grip on my knee tightens, her warmth pulling me back from the void I've been staring into for months. It's grounding but also terrifying because what if I can't come back all the way? What if it's already too late?

"Oscar," she says again, her voice a fragile thread of emotion, "I'm not asking you to face this alone. I don't care how bad it is or how deep it goes. We're in this together. You have to let me help you."

For a moment, I just sit there, absorbing her words, feeling the love and desperation woven into every syllable. Her eyes are pleading, filled with the kind of hope that I thought had been shattered long ago. And God, I want to believe that she can help, that we can fix this. Fix me.

A darker, more insidious voice whispers that hope is a luxury I can't afford.

"What if there's nothing left of me to save?" I ask, barely recognizing the voice that comes out of my mouth.

It's not a question I ever thought I'd ask, but it's been gnawing at me since that crash. Since everything inside me started to shift and change into something I don't understand.

Sierra's eyes glisten with unshed tears, but she doesn't shy away. Her grip on my knee is as determined as ever, steadying me.

"Then we'll find you again," she says. "We'll rebuild. I don't care how long it takes, or how hard it is. You're still my Oscar, and I refuse to lose you. Not to this. Not to anything."

The raw, unfiltered emotion in her words is like a lifeline, pulling me back from the precipice just enough for me to feel a semblance of solid ground beneath my feet. It's enough to break through the fog, if only for a moment.

"I don't know where to start," I finally admit, my voice shaking. It's the first honest truth I've spoken in weeks, if not months. Admitting it feels like ripping off a bandage that's been left on for too long, but beneath it, the wound festers, raw and unhealed.

"Start with me," Sierra says softly, her thumb tracing slow circles on my knee. "Start by letting me in, by telling me everything you're feeling—no matter how messy or painful it is. We can't fix this on our own terms if you're building walls."

Her words offer solace, but the weariness in her voice doesn't go unnoticed. She's tired, too, fighting her own invisible battles alongside mine. But it's clearer now. This is not just my burden to carry.

"There's this ... noise, in my head," I hear myself say, the words spilling out before I can second-guess them. "It's like a constant hum, but not something you'd hear with your ears —more like a feeling. It's always there, driving me mad. And then the flashes of things that I know aren't mine. I see places I've never been to, people I've never met. But they're so real, Sierra, like I lived them."

She listens intently, her focus unwavering, as though desperately searching for a thread she can hold onto—something that will start to make sense in all this chaos.

"And sometimes, I feel like I'm being watched," I continue, my jaw tensing. "Not like a paranoia-filled freak-out, but something more subtle. Like whoever they are, they're waiting for ... something. A moment, a trigger, I don't know. But it's there, a lingering presence that I can't shake."

Sierra's brows furrow, processing each word until she finally speaks. I know it's hard for her to separate her training as a clinical psychologist with her role as a wife. I hope she sees me as more than a patient or a test subject. I think she does.

"When you say *they*, who do you mean? Do you know who they are?" she asks.

The questions rattle me, shaking the last bit of resolve I'm clinging to. I run my fingers through my short hair, trying to hold on to the edges of my fraying sanity.

"I don't know. I don't know if it's real or if I'm losing my mind, but it feels real. And then there's this ... darkness."

"Darkness?"

"Yeah, like a void. It's hard to explain, but it feels ... alive, sentient. It grows every time I think about it, every time I try to make sense of these flashes or try to piece together the things I see. It's like it wants to consume me whole."

Sierra's face pales, and I can see the fear in her eyes mirroring my own. She believes me. Yet, she doesn't pull away. If anything, she shifts closer, her knee touching mine. I have to give her credit. She's handling this as well as could be expected.

"Oscar, this sounds like it could be related to the crash, some form of trauma—or maybe even a neurological condition like I mentioned earlier," she says carefully, her voice calm despite the alarm evident in her expression. "But if you're feeling like this ... if you believe there's something more to it, we need to explore every possibility."

Her hand moves from my knee to cover my hand, squeezing it gently. "We're going to figure this out, but you have to trust me. Okay? Can you do that?"

I want to—I really do. But as much as I need her support, there's also a gnawing certainty within me that tells me that whatever's happening can't be fixed with therapy or medication. This is something else, something that goes beyond the physical or psychological.

Something deeper, more sinister.

How do I explain that to her without sounding completely insane? Especially since I can't be sure that my mind isn't playing tricks on me.

"I'm scared," I finally admit, my voice barely above a whisper. "Scared that if we dig too deep, we might uncover something we can't undo. And we'll both be pulled into it."

Her eyes soften, and she leans in closer, bringing both hands up to cradle my face. "Listen, there isn't a single thing you could tell me that would make me want to leave you. We get through this, no matter how dark it gets. We've faced tough times before. This is no different."

Her touch, the warmth of her hands, it grounds me. The fog briefly clears, and for a second, I feel like the old Oscar—the Oscar who could face anything as long as Sierra was by his side.

Yet, there's a shadow lingering at the edge of my consciousness, a cold, creeping doubt that ties my stomach into knots. This is scarier and more serious than anything we've been through before.

"Okay," I manage to say, my voice steadying just slightly. "Okay, but I need you to promise me something."

She tilts her head, her eyes filled with love and worry. "Anything."

"If, at any point, this gets too much—if something happens to me or I hurt you, I need you to protect yourself. Don't let yourself get dragged under. Don't let whatever this is consume you, too."

Her eyes widen, and for a moment, she doesn't speak. I

can see the internal struggle written across her face—part of her wanting to dismiss it immediately, to reassure me that we'll face this together, no matter what. But the other part—the pragmatic, self-preserving part—knows I might be right. That there's a risk, a darkness, that could very well swallow us both if left unchecked.

"I don't want to think about that," she finally whispers, her voice fragile. "But if it makes you feel better, then I promise. I'll protect myself."

Her words should bring me relief, but instead, they feel like a door closing—a door I hoped would never have to be opened. Even as she makes the promise, I can see the determination in her eyes, the unspoken vow that she's not going anywhere, no matter how bad this gets. She might have said the words, but I know Sierra. She's stubborn and fiercely loyal. She'll fight for me until there's nothing left of her.

That's what scares me the most. It fucking terrifies me.

For a while, we sit there in silence. It's as if we're both trying to grasp the enormity of what we're facing, but the shape of it remains elusive.

I finally look up, meeting her gaze, and I see the same haunted fear mirrored in her eyes, mingled with the deepest resolve. I know she'll stand by me, no matter what comes, but the thought of dragging her into this darkness feels like the greatest betrayal.

I hate myself for what I'm doing to her.

"We'll get through this," she repeats, her voice just a little stronger, like she's trying to convince herself as much as me.

I nod, not trusting myself to speak. Instead, I reach out and pull her into an embrace, holding her close against my chest, the steady rhythm of her heartbeat calming the storm of thoughts swirling in my mind. There's a comfort in the closeness, in the familiar scent of her long, wavy hair, the warmth of her body pressed against mine.

For a moment, the world could be normal. We could be okay.

But deep down, I know this is only the beginning of our troubles.

As we sit there, entwined on the couch in the darkness of our living room, I feel the silence growing.

Chapter Seven

SIERRA

I hold Oscar tight, feeling the warmth of his body seep into mine, but the terror behind his words lingers in the air around us, cold and numbing.

This is the man I promised to stand beside for better or worse, but the worse I imagined never came close to this. I thought we were going to face the usual struggles—arguments over finances, the strain of dual careers, the agony of being separated by deployments. I never thought I'd have to fight to keep him tethered to reality, to anchor him while he drifts further into the unknown.

My mind drifts and I remember a time when we'd first started dating. Oscar had come to Quantico for Officer Candidate School, which meant we didn't see each other for ten weeks. It felt like an eternity. There was a break halfway through for weekend liberty, and I drove up from Atlanta so that we could spend the weekend together. I rented a hotel room and we spent most of our time in bed, curled around each other eating takeout and watching movies—when we weren't making love. There was something wild in Oscar's eyes that I hadn't noticed before then. He looked ragged and thin, even when he put on his dress blues for a night out at a fancy restaurant. I got the impression that he'd seen and done things he'd never speak of to me.

That was the first time I got a sense of what life as a Marine Corps officer's wife would be like. Only this? What's happening now? That weekend and its realization doesn't hold a candle to the gravity of our current situation.

Oscar's breath is warm against my neck, the solid pressure of his arms around me grounding us both, but my mind can't stop whirling with a million questions. Who is the *they* he mentioned? And what did he mean when he said they might have done something to him? Dark scenarios play out in my head, each more insidious than the last. None provides any real answers.

All I know is that I can't lose him. Not like this.

"Come to bed," I murmur, my voice barely louder than a whisper. I turn my face slightly, pressing my lips against his temple, trying to convey through that simple gesture what words can't.

Oscar remains motionless for a moment before nodding slowly, the weariness in his body finally bleeding into his mind, too. It drags him down. I take his hand and lead him from the living room to our bedroom, where the bed looms like a vast chasm between us and whatever lies ahead.

Inside, I feel the overwhelming urge to keep him safe, to wrap him up in my arms and protect him from the tempest raging inside his mind. But what if the threat isn't something I can even see, let alone fend off?

We strip down in silence, going through the nightly motions in a kind of detached rhythm, our usual routine now heavy with the weight of everything unspoken. I slide under the duvet, the cool sheets a sharp contrast to the warmth of the room. Oscar hesitates for a heartbeat before joining me, his movements slow and deliberate, as though he might shatter at any moment.

I turn on my side to face him, letting my hand rest against his chest, feeling the steady, reassuring thrum of his heartbeat beneath my palm. I want to tell him how much I love him and how much I need him to stay with me, but the words are trapped in my throat.

He turns slightly, placing his hand over mine as he locks eyes with me. There's a desperate, haunted look in his eyes, and for a moment, I wonder if touching him like this makes it worse. His chest rises and falls under my hand, and I can see the battle warring inside him. He wants to hold on to something real, something tethered, while his mind drifts into the shadows.

"I don't want to lose you," I whisper, my voice trembling with barely contained emotion. "Not tonight. Not ever."

His gaze softens, the anguish melting into something raw. Something that makes my heart wrench with equal parts love and pain.

"You won't," he says, but there's a fragility in his voice that betrays him. "But if I'm going to lose control, there's one thing I need to hold on to."

He shifts closer to me, and without another word, his lips find mine. The kiss starts out tentative and gentle. A brush of warmth, of need. Soon, it deepens and becomes more urgent, as if he's clinging to this moment, to the sensation of being grounded, of still being *Oscar* with me.

"I love you, you know?" I whisper.

"I know. I love you, too."

There's something frantic in the way his hands move over my body, as though he's trying to memorize every curve, every contour. Like he's afraid tomorrow might steal it all away.

I respond in kind, my hands tracing familiar paths over his chest, his shoulders, pulling him closer, needing him closer. It's not just about sex. Not tonight. This is about connection, about trust, about holding on to something that feels real amidst all the fear and confusion.

As his hands move lower, slipping beneath my nightgown, I arch into his touch, the sensation sending a shiver throughout my body. I close my eyes, letting myself get lost in the way his fingertips caress my skin, the way he holds his breath when he senses my reaction. There's a beat of silence, an unspoken hesitation, and then his hand stills against my waist.

"Sierra ..." He murmurs my name like a prayer.

I cup his face with my hands, bringing his gaze back to mine, giving him a nod of reassurance. "I'm here," I say against his lips, kissing him again, deeper this time. For all the times I've tried to comfort him, I realize that this might be the only real way to bring him back—even if just for a moment.

Sexual healing is real.

He presses closer, his lips feverish against mine, and in this moment, there's no trauma, no fear. Just us. His hands slide up my back, pulling me against him as if he can merge our bodies in a desperate attempt to make sure I won't slip away from him. The urgency, the need, it's all there, but there's tenderness too, a desperate kind of gentleness that only someone near their breaking point can possess. As if by being too rough, he might shatter what little we have left.

Oscar's breath mingles with mine, shallow but intense, as he rolls us slightly so that I'm beneath him. His weight is reassuring, not oppressive, but grounding in a way that neither of us can put into words. His lips leave mine just long enough to trail down my neck, the warmth sending tremors through my body. Each touch is laden with a silent plea. A reminder of what's at stake. Of everything we're fighting for and everything we could lose.

I gasp as his movements become more deliberate, more focused. He's not just touching me. He's *worshipping* me, like I'm the only thing connecting him to this world.

His hand trails lower, slipping between us, and I can't help the way my body responds, needing this closeness as much as he does.

Sometimes, since the crash, he has trouble getting an erection. When he presses against me, strong and unyielding, I breathe a sigh of relief. It makes me feel loved and wanted. It makes me remember the good times.

My breath hitches as his fingers find the sensitive skin just beneath my waistband, drawing out a moan that I've been holding back. In this moment, nothing else matters. Not the fear, the uncertainty, the nightmarish spirals.

Just this. Just him.

"How do you do that?" he murmurs against my skin, his voice thick with desire and something deeper that I can't quite place. His fingers slide over me, gentle yet relentless, just enough to stir a fire deep within me.

"Do what?" I manage, barely coherent, as I arch into his touch, needing more of him, needing to drag him out of that void with everything I have.

"Make me feel ... anything," he whispers, his words raw

and jagged, like they've been torn from somewhere deep inside him. "Make me feel like I'm still here."

I can't find the words to respond, but I don't need to. My actions speak for me, the way I close the small distance still between our bodies and press myself against him, seeking to erase all the space, all the doubts, with our connection. I reach down, guiding him as he shudders in response to my touch. There's an intensity in the way he looks at me—an anchor in the wild storm of confusion and fear that he's been lost in.

With a tenderness that borders on desperation, he kisses me again, his lips traveling from my mouth to my neck, down to my collarbone, making me tremble in a way that's charged with raw emotion.

This isn't merely physical—this is a reminder that we are still here. Still us. Still together.

His hands roam over me, mapping every inch of my body as though he's memorizing it anew, his warmth melding into mine as he lowers himself closer, his weight and strength pressing against me. His breath is ragged, and I can feel his pulse thrumming under the surface where our bodies touch. It quickens as he enters me with a gentle, deliberate movement that sends sparks through every nerve in my body.

Oscar moans softly against my ear, his mouth finding my lips again. There's an urgency in the way he moves, a rhythm that builds with each thrust as if he's trying to outrun something.

I match him, holding him close, my fingers digging into his back as I draw him deeper. We lose ourselves in the physical, the raw emotion of it all—the need to connect in the most elemental way possible. Each sigh, each moan, each ragged breath pulls us further from the abyss.

The world narrows until there's nothing but the two of us.

The slow burn of desire unfurls in the pit of my stomach, spreading like wildfire through my veins. The doubt fades, replaced by the overwhelming sensation of being lost in this man. The man I love. The man I refuse to lose to the shadows that have been closing in around us.

His movements become more insistent, and I meet him pace for pace, our breath tangling together in a chaotic symphony that demands release. The bed creaks beneath us, a stark contrast to the silence of the night outside. As the intensity builds, my body tightens around him. When the final thread snaps, it releases us both into a shared wave of pleasure that crashes down like a tidal wave.

In that instant, everything falls away. There is only this moment, suspended in time, where we are whole, where I am with Oscar and Oscar is with me.

As the climax fades, we collapse into each other, breathless and trembling, riding out the aftershocks in the silence that follows. His body is warm and solid against mine, and I cling to it with everything I have left.

For several long moments, there's nothing but the sound of our slowing breaths, mingled together in the quiet of the night. His weight on top of me is comforting, grounding me in a reality where we're not lost. I can feel his heart pounding, slowly but surely returning to a steady rhythm beneath my hand.

Oscar pulls back slightly, his forehead resting against mine, and I close my eyes, savoring the closeness. This is the man I know. The man I love. The man I've fought so hard to protect, even as he drifts further from me with each passing day.

When I open my eyes, I find him staring down at me with a raw vulnerability that stirs something deep within. In that gaze, I see not just the man who's been slipping away from me, but also the fight within him. There's a desperate need to stay, to hold on, even as the darkness threatens to pull him under.

"I'm still here," he whispers hoarsely, his voice cracking, as if trying to convince himself as much as me.

I cradle his face in my hands, thumbs brushing the stubble along his jaw, and press my lips to his forehead. "Yes, you are."

He rests his head against my bare chest, his shoulders sagging with a weariness that tugs at my heart. Slowly, his hands begin to relax their grip, his trembling easing as he allows himself to be held—just held—within the comfort of my embrace.

We lie there in the darkness, the warmth of our bodies tangled beneath the blankets, trying to absorb what just happened. We both wonder what it means and whether it's enough to keep us fighting.

I can't shake the feeling that something ominous still looms, like a cloud of darkness just beyond the walls of our home. For now, I force myself to push it aside.

Chapter Eight

OSCAR

The warmth of Sierra's embrace was supposed to be grounding, something to anchor me in the chaos that was my mind. It was. Sort of.

As I lie next to her, though, our breaths slowing to a synchronized rhythm in the darkness, the sense of peace I crave remains elusive. The fog that shrouds my thoughts thickens, curling tighter around my brain until I can feel the pressure of it like a vice.

Damn it.

I tell myself to focus on her—on the steady rise and fall of her chest, on the soft beat of her heart beneath my palm. I nuzzle into the curve of her neck, her skin still carrying the warmth of our shared intimacy. Yet, the closer I try to hold onto this moment, the further it seems to slip away. I can feel something clawing at the edges of my thoughts. It's a sharp, gnawing sensation that refuses to let me rest.

I've had such a hard time sleeping lately. I'm certain the lack of sleep is only exacerbating my problems.

Sierra stirs, shifting her weight slightly to get comfortable.

As her arm brushes over mine, I suddenly feel a jolt of irritation spike through my body, quick and bright like electricity. It's ridiculous—*this anger*—over something minor and inconsequential. The sensation is real, though, as if her touch has ignited a short-circuit within me. The warmth I'd been clinging to a second ago has transformed into something that sears. Something that makes me want to push her away.

I take a slow, controlled breath, trying to brush it off. It's nothing—or at least, it should be nothing. She's not doing anything wrong. *I'm* the one who's off.

Despite my wish for it to go away, the prickling in my skin remains. It's a burning heat that neither intimacy nor mental will can banish.

I roll slightly onto my back, letting my arm slide off her and creating a sliver of space between us. It's meant to be comforting. Instead, it feels like a buffer between the real me and whatever is festering beneath the surface. Sierra doesn't seem to notice and lets out a soft sigh, curling unconsciously toward the pillow beside her.

Just relax, I tell myself. *You're being irrational. You need sleep—real sleep—maybe that will help.*

As I close my eyes, trying to will my body into submission, the buzzing in my head persists, more insistent. I can feel my heartbeat hammering in my chest, and the irritation soon gives way to a restless energy that has nowhere to go. It paces within me like a caged animal, clawing at my insides, demanding release.

I shift again, more forcefully this time, which causes the bed to creak beneath my weight. Sierra stirs but doesn't fully wake, simply mumbling something unintelligible before sinking back into her slumber.

I tell myself to calm down—to breathe, just breathe—but the irritation within me only builds in intensity. It's irrational, I know, but my mind seizes upon the noise of her breathing. The steady, rhythmic sound that usually soothes me now grates against my nerves. I feel myself getting angrier for no reason, like there's some unseen force stoking the flames inside me.

I roll out of bed carefully, trying not to wake her, and pace the length of our bedroom, running a hand through my hair. I need to shake this off.

Why won't it just go away?

The thoughts swirl faster and faster, an inescapable cyclone that pulls me deeper into my own frustrations.

Suddenly, a flash of memory hits me—an image of Sierra's hurt expression during our conversation earlier in the evening, and that look of fear in her eyes when I told her about the darkness inside me. My fists clench involuntarily. I shouldn't be feeling this way—toward her of all people. She's my wife. She's the only one who's tried to help me.

Another image flickers—the man who came into that spare room on the base—his face, his cryptic words, they all begin to blur together with this anger I can't seem to escape.

I have to get control.

This isn't me.

Even though I'm telling myself this, there's a hard pit of rage in my stomach, a boiling heat that needs an outlet. Any outlet.

I take another involuntary step forward toward the bed, feeling the anger rise again—and then without thinking, I slam my fist down on the nightstand next to it.

The sound echoes unbearably loud in the quiet room,

slicing through the somber atmosphere like jagged glass. In the aftermath, I feel a rush of fear lance through me.

What the hell did I just do?

It's too late. The damage is done.

Sierra bolts upright, eyes wide and disoriented from sleep, her breath catching in her throat as she takes in the scene. Her gaze jumps from my fist on the splintered wood to my face, her expression transforming from confusion to fear in a split second.

I see it—the stark terror that crosses her features, and it's like a bucket of ice water dumped over my head. The anger, the overwhelming urge to destroy something, anything, vanishes in an instant, leaving behind a suffocating wave of guilt and shame.

"Sierra ..." I start, stepping back, raising my hands as if to show her I mean no harm. But she's already scooting further away, pulling the duvet tighter around her as if it could act as some sort of shield. Her eyes never leave mine. They're wide and unblinking, as though she's struggling to process what just happened. What I just did.

"Oscar, what ... what just happened?" she stammers, voice trembling.

Her fear is palpable in the room. I've never seen her like this.

"I'm sorry," I whisper, barely able to meet her gaze. My voice sounds alien to my own ears, broken and raw. "I don't know what came over me."

She doesn't respond immediately, her eyes darting to the shattered wood of the nightstand, then back to me, as if she's trying to reconcile the man she knows with the violent outburst she just witnessed.

I take a cautious step toward the bed, but she shifts away, her movement instinctive, defensive. The look of fear on her face twists something deep inside me, something that's already bruised and bleeding. I force myself to stop.

"I would never hurt you," I say, desperation clawing at my throat as I try to make her understand. "You know that, right? You have to believe me. I would never—"

"I know," she cuts in, though her voice is as brittle as glass about to break. "But I've never seen you like this. What's happening to you?"

Her words are a plea, a desperate call for reassurance, for some semblance of the man she married to still be in there. But how can I give her what she needs when I don't even recognize myself anymore?

I run a hand over my face, trying to wrangle my thoughts into some semblance of order while the weight of her gaze presses down on me like the full gravity of a planet.

"I wish I had an answer, Sierra. I wish I could tell you what's happening, but I—" My voice breaks, and I feel something inside me finally crack under the pressure I've been carrying for so long. "I don't know. Maybe I'm broken in ways no one can fix."

Tears well in Sierra's eyes, and I see the pain behind them. Pain that I've caused, even inadvertently. The thought is enough to make my stomach churn with guilt. I keep replaying the moment over and over—my fist slamming down, her reaction, the jarring sound of wood splintering filling the room. It's becoming a nightmare on loop in the back of my mind.

For a moment, the room teeters between silence and words neither of us know how to say.

Then Sierra slowly takes a breath and I see her force herself to be still. Her fear melts into determination as her eyes harden with resolution. She isn't backing down, and I realize that, despite everything, she's still fighting for me. For us.

I can hardly believe it. This woman is incredible.

"We're going to get through this," she says, her voice steady but soft. "But you need to see how serious this is. We can't ignore what's happening to you."

Only the slightest wobble in her voice betrays the strength she's trying to muster. I want to hold her and assure her that everything will be okay, but the truth is, I don't know if it will be. I don't know if the man I've become is capable of saving us.

It's possible that I'm already too far gone.

Sierra glances warily at the shattered furniture before returning her gaze to me, and I see the hint of tears she's trying to blink away. "I love you. But I'm scared—terrified really—of what's happening. Do I need to call someone?"

Her plea rends something deep inside me. The pit of anger that had powered my actions just minutes earlier crumbles into a void of sorrow. "Sierra," I start, voice strangled, "I'm afraid, too. I don't want to be like this ... I don't want to hurt you in any way. I don't want you to feel like you have to call someone. But I don't know how to make it stop."

She reaches out, cautiously, bridging the distance between us with her hand, placing it gently on the arm that's still trembling from the impact with the nightstand.

Her touch, tentative but warm, eases some of the tension coiled inside me.

I lower myself slowly onto the bed beside her, careful not

to make any sudden movements that might reignite her fear. Her touch, normally a comfort, feels fragile now. As though the slightest misstep could sever the connection between us.

We sit in silence, the only sound the soft rustle of the duvet as she adjusts it around her shoulders, shielding herself from more than just the cool night air. I can feel her gaze on me, like she's searching for something, anything, that can bring back the man she once knew.

"I know I said it before. I really don't want to lose you," she finally whispers, her voice cracking under the weight of her emotions. "I can't do this alone, though. I need you to meet me halfway. If you need help, you need to call someone. Let them help us."

Her words cut deep, exposing the bare truth of our situation. I know she's right—this can't go on. The path I'm on will destroy us both, if I let it. But how do I fight a battle when I don't even know who or what I'm up against?

"I never wanted you to carry this, Sierra," I reply, my voice hoarse with the strain of holding back the flood of emotions. "I never wanted you to see me like this, to be afraid of me. But I don't know how to keep it from you anymore."

Her eyes soften, and for a moment, I see a flicker of the love that has always been there between us. The love that has weathered deployments, distance, and now this.

"We'll figure something out," she says, her voice filled with a determination that almost makes me believe her. "We have to."

I want to believe that she's right, but deep down, a part of me wonders if this is beyond anything we've faced before. Something that we're not equipped to survive.

Sierra shifts closer, placing her other hand on mine, her

grip both comforting and demanding. "Promise me," she says, her voice trembling slightly, "promise me you won't shut me out. Even when it gets bad, even when you think you're protecting me, I need to be in this with you."

Her plea is a lifeline, but it's also a burden. How can I shield her from the chaos?

I'm not sure that I can.

Chapter Nine

SIERRA

His promise feels like a fragile infusion of hope, a thin thread of light. I hold onto it, needing to believe that we can pull through this, even if the path forward remains unclear.

For tonight, we manage to settle back into the bed, our bodies curled together, still hyperaware of the unease lingering. I cling to him, hoping that through sheer will and love, I can keep him from slipping away. As we lie here, though, the unease within me grows, gnawing at the foundation of my trust. The man I'm holding is my husband, but something has taken root inside him.

What if I'm not safe with him? The thought is terrible and scary, but it's there. I can't deny it to myself. If asked, I'm not sure how well I could deny it to someone else, either.

Morning comes too quickly, bringing with it the cold light of another gray winter day. It filters through the blinds, casting pale slants of light across the room and pulling us out of the cocoon of closeness we tried to preserve through the night. Oscar stirs beside me, his muscles tense, his face lined with the torment that seems to have etched itself into his features.

I watch him as he sits up, running a hand through his short hair, the skin around his eyes a little darker, sharper. The stress of last night makes each movement appear labored, as though he's carrying something too heavy to bear.

I'm reluctant to speak, but I force myself to say something. "Did you sleep at all?"

He doesn't answer right away, his jaw working as he stares at some fixed point ahead. Finally, he shakes his head. "Not really."

There's so much more I want to ask, but I can't bring myself to voice the questions. I'm too afraid of pushing him further away. I know there's a line we've been walking, a line that feels thinner every day, and I'm terrified of what will happen if we cross it.

"I'm sorry," I say simply.

Oscar swings his legs over the edge of the bed, his feet landing softly on the hardwood floor. He stands up slowly, almost reluctantly. A few silent moments pass, and I watch as he crosses to the bathroom. His movements are careful, deliberate, as if he's avoiding triggering something. The door closes behind him with a soft click, leaving me alone with my thoughts. The faint sound of running water is the only thing grounding me in the present.

My mind churns with a thousand worries, each one more unsettling than the last.

What am I supposed to do now? How do I help someone who's spiraling into a place I can't follow?

I think about texting Beth, but I don't want to anger Oscar by sharing his personal troubles with someone else. I might still talk to her about this, but I feel like I should, at least, have that conversation in person. I'm sure she has plenty to say about what she witnessed at dinner last night.

It's embarrassing.

I push back the covers, feeling the chill of the morning air on my skin, and pad across the room to the spot where Oscar's fist had shattered the nightstand. The wood is splintered. Jagged edges jut out like exposed nerves. It's a physical manifestation of the rage that had surged through my husband only hours ago.

Our bedroom furniture once belonged to my grandparents. My mom and dad had it refinished and gave it to us as a gift when we got married. I'm sad to see it damaged.

I reach out to touch the broken surface, feeling the raw edges bite into my fingertips. It's almost impossible to reconcile this violence with the man I love. After all, Oscar is the man who once built a bookcase by hand for our first apartment. His touch was so gentle. So precise.

The thought makes my heart twist painfully in my chest.

The memory of his promises last night offers a fragile thread of hope, one I cling to with everything I have. He hasn't given up on us yet. That means I can't either.

The sound of the shower stops, and I step back from the nightstand, quickly brushing the splinters from my hand. I don't want Oscar to see me studying the damage. Instead, I move to the closet to find something to wear, pretending as though it's just an ordinary morning.

Nothing about this feels ordinary anymore.

When Oscar re-emerges from the bathroom, there's a strained silence between us. He's dressed in his usual dark jeans and a sweater—his uniform when he's not actually in uniform. His expression is carefully neutral, but I can see the unrest behind his eyes.

I force a smile. "I was thinking I'd make some coffee. Want some?"

He hesitates, then nods slowly. "Yeah, that sounds good."

I disappear into the kitchen, grateful for the chance to busy myself with the routine of brewing coffee. The familiar sounds—the soft hiss of the coffee machine, the rattle of cups—help to ground me. My hands tremble as I go through the motions.

As I wait for the coffee to finish brewing, I glance back toward the living room, catching a glimpse of Oscar leaning against the doorframe. His posture is relaxed, yet the tension in his shoulders tells a different story—a contradiction that makes my heart ache.

"Do you want to talk about last night?" I ask cautiously, turning my attention back to the machine. I can hear the bubbling of the coffee as it brews, each gurgle echoing the uncertainty that weighs heavily in the air.

He exhales slowly, taking a long breath that sounds almost resigned. "Honestly?" he replies, and I can tell he's struggling to harness the right words, to find a way to express what he's feeling. "I don't."

I turn around to face him, resting my hands against the counter for support. "I think we should talk about it. We can take it slow. Just answer what you feel comfortable with, okay? I think we both know that we can't ignore what happened."

After a long moment, he finally steps into the kitchen, moving closer but not quite closing the distance. "I didn't mean to scare you," he says, his voice low and heavy with frustration. "When I punched the nightstand, it wasn't about you or—" He runs a hand over his face, as if trying to wipe away the remnants of confusion and pain clinging to him. "I lost control. It just ... happened."

"I know," I say softly, taking a step toward him. "But it's not just about last night, Oscar. There's something else happening—something between us that's shifting, and if we don't address it, I'm scared it could get worse."

He runs a hand through his hair again, the gesture both anxious and familiar. "I feel like I'm fighting a battle on two fronts. One, I'm trying to figure out why the hell I can't seem to breathe inside my own head. And two, I'm trying to hold onto you. You're the only thing that feels real anymore."

Hearing him say that stirs something inside me. "I'm right here, Oscar. You're not going to lose me." I take another step forward, closing the gap just enough so that I can reach for his hand, intertwining our fingers. "When you lashed out, it scared me."

His gaze softens for a brief moment as my fingers wrap around his, but then something flickers across his face—an internal battle playing out behind those stormy eyes. Just as I think he might push forward, the tension coils tighter, choking off the moment.

"I appreciate your concern, but I can't deal with this right now," he says abruptly, pulling his hand away and stepping back. There's an urgency in him that I can't understand.

I don't like it.

"Where are you going?" I ask, bewildered. "We need to talk about this, Oscar!"

"It's the weekend, Sierra," he replies. "We don't have to face this now. I need some air."

Before I can respond, he's out the door, the sound of his footsteps echoing through the house. Left alone, my heart sinks.

Why can't we confront it together? I was taught to talk through problems. I don't know any other way.

I grab my phone, a desperate impulse guiding me to reach out to someone who might understand. I scroll through my contacts, pausing with my finger hovering over Beth's name. Even though I know she cares, I hesitate, unsure if she can handle this or if she has the emotional bandwidth to help. Besides, she might have already seen too much at dinner last night.

Instead, I tap on Brian Kennedy, a college buddy who's a social worker. He knows a bit about trauma, and maybe he can suggest something for Oscar that will keep him from slipping further into whatever dark void he's fighting. In the back of my mind, I hear the echoes of Oscar's last words about needing to breathe.

"Sierra! It's good to hear from you," Brian picks up, his voice warm and steady. I feel a flicker of comfort at the sound.

"Hey, Brian," I reply, forcing a calm. "I didn't know if you'd be available, but I could really use your advice."

"Of course! What's on your mind?"

I take a deep breath, trying to navigate the delicate labyrinth of my thoughts. "It's about Oscar. He's been acting different—erratic, and honestly, a little scary. Last night, he lost control and punched a hole in the nightstand."

There's a pause on the other end of the line, and I can almost hear the wheels turning in Brian's mind. "Wow," he finally says, his tone shifting to one of concern. "That sounds serious. How's he handling it?"

I chew on the inside of my cheek, struggling to find the right words. "He says he doesn't remember much about it, but he feels like he's losing control. Like he can't connect with himself—or with me." My voice trembles on the last part, revealing just how fragile I feel.

"Has he been violent toward you?"

I hesitate. My inclination is to say yes, which is interesting because it's not true. It's almost like I sense that he will be violent toward me in the future.

"No," I finally say. "His anger isn't directed at me."

Brian lets out a soft sigh. "Sierra, I get that this is alarming, but sometimes stress manifests in strange and unpredictable ways, especially with someone in Oscar's position. Maybe he's just overwhelmed," he offers, attempting to downplay the seriousness. "I remember you telling me when you first met that Oscar and his friends had gotten rowdy at a wetdown. Didn't one of the guys get into a fight with a bartender? Do you remember that?"

"Yes, of course I do, but this is more than just stress," I rush to explain, desperation leaking into my tone. "I've been watching him change—his moods, his reactions, everything. It feels like he's battling something deeper, something he can't even explain. I'm worried he's hurting. And for the record, Oscar didn't fight anyone at that wetdown. I've always seen him as more refined than most Marines."

"Have you considered that he might need some professional help?" Brian suggests gently, though his voice still echoes with a hint of skepticism. "Sometimes it's hard for people to admit they need support. It can take time. Be patient with him."

"Patient? He's shutting me out. How am I supposed to be patient while he's spiraling?"

I can hear the irritation creeping into my voice, and I rub my forehead, willing the tension to dissipate. "I'm sorry, if I sound short. I need someone to understand that I feel helpless. I can't let my husband fall apart like this."

"I do understand," Brian replies, his voice steady, though I can sense he's shifting back into that counselor role. While comforting, it makes it difficult to share my raw fears. "You have to remember, though, that all you can do is encourage him to seek help. As his partner, your support is invaluable, but you can't force him to confront something he's not ready for. It's a journey, and he might need to come to that realization himself."

I close my eyes and lean against the kitchen counter, wishing for a clearer path forward. "What if it gets worse?" I murmur.

"You take things one step at a time. It's a lot to handle, and it's okay if you feel overwhelmed, too."

I'm less than impressed. In fact, I feel dismissed. I didn't expect this from Brian. Come to think of it, I felt a similar vibe from Beth at dinner last night. People seem to want to distance themselves from this. To brush it off, glad they aren't the ones having to deal with it up close and personal.

I hang up the phone with a sense of frustration swirling within me. Brian, with all his training and experience, doesn't seem to grasp the enormity of what I'm facing. The way he suggested that I simply *support* Oscar felt dismissive, as if I were overreacting. Perhaps it's easier for him to stay compartmentalized in his office, providing advice without the emotional investment I have in my husband.

I think about it for a while as I buzz around the house doing miscellaneous chores. Finally, I decide to reach out to my parents. Maybe they'll understand. Maybe they can provide some wisdom to help me navigate this dark chapter. I hit dial and wait, feeling a mix of hope and anxiety. It rings a few times before my mother picks up.

"Hello? Sierra, honey! How are you?" her cheerful voice envelops me, and for a moment, I feel a slice of comfort.

"I'm okay, Mom," I reply, attempting to mask my worries. "How's the weather in Savannah?"

"Warm and sunny, as usual," she says. "Although, it is cooler than your dad would prefer. He won't get in the pool this time of year. Not until the outside temps are at least eighty degrees. You know how he is."

It must be nice to have such simple problems. I sigh. I'm happy that they're happy, but *wow*. How will they begin to understand my situation? Jen and Marty Mallory have been married for more than thirty years. It's a good marriage, too. Not one of those fake ones where the couple avoids each other and lives separate lives.

"I wanted to talk to you and Dad about Oscar."

"Oh, sweetheart, what about him?" Mom asks, the warmth still lacing her tone.

"He's been acting differently since the helicopter crash," I begin. "I'm really worried about him. Last night, he lost control and punched a hole in the nightstand. He seems so distant, and I don't know how to help him."

There's a pause on the other end, and I can imagine her processing my words, maybe even feeling the sting of concern for her daughter.

"Oh honey, don't be silly," she finally says, her voice light.

"He's just adjusting. These things happen, especially with stressful jobs. You know how military men can be. Just give him some time. Men don't always show it, but they have their ways of coping. You'll see, he'll be back to normal in no time."

"Mom, it's not just a phase," I push, my frustration seeping through. "This isn't just common stress. He seems like a completely different person. What if it gets worse? What if he hurts himself or someone else? He's losing control."

"Mmm, maybe some more time in the field will do him good," she suggests, brushing aside my fears like a pesky mosquito. "He'll settle back into his routine. You need to be more understanding, Sierra, dear. Stress can do funny things to a man, but you can't underestimate his resilience. Just be there for him, sweetie."

I bite my tongue. I decide not to wait for my dad to get on the phone. I suspect he'll tell me more of the same.

"Thanks, Mom," I say. "Tell Dad I had to go. I'll call back another time."

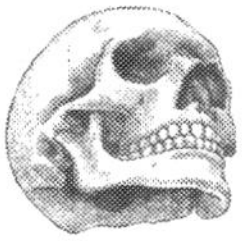

Chapter Ten

OSCAR

Monday morning arrives and I sit alone at my desk, the faint hum of the fluorescent lights overhead distracting me from the torrent of thoughts swirling in my head. A potent mix of frustration and confusion floods my mind, overshadowing everything else.

Today is supposed to be different. I've been telling myself that all weekend.

I channel my energy into the work in front of me, trying to drown out the rest. There's been talk of sending me to Djibouti for a few months. I'd appreciate the opportunity to get away, but I'll admit that I have concerns about my ability to perform the required duties. Perhaps it would be best to send someone else in my place. I haven't said that to General Benedict yet. I'm not sure if I should.

With every tick of the clock, the pressure builds. My fingers drum anxiously against the hard surface of the desk, a mechanical echo that seems to taunt my inability to pinpoint what's happening inside of me. I take a breath, trying to steady myself, but it feels like inhaling cold air laced with static electricity. It's suffocating.

That flash of anger from Friday night becomes a specter, a reminder of how quickly shadows can surface when I least expect them. What the hell is wrong with me? I've spent so many hours analyzing the events leading up to the crash—the decision-making, the fear, the weight of lives on my shoulders—but none of it seemed to matter when I smashed my fist into the nightstand.

I glance at the half-empty glass of water beside my computer. Uneasiness claws at my insides. I can't work like this. I need to clear my head. I push back my chair and head for the small window, trying to breathe in the crisp air that pushes through the cracked opening.

The office is unusually quiet, the kind of stillness that feels anticipatory. But I'm not listening to the silence. I'm wrestling with the uncomfortable truth of my disposition—a battle between regret and the primal urge to lash out.

"Control yourself," I murmur to my reflection in the glass. "You can't keep doing this." But even as I say it, the unresolved tension inside me gnaws at my resolve, rendering me a prisoner in my own skin.

I step back, rubbing my temples as I turn away from the window, too tired and frustrated to keep wrestling with myself. I decide to grab some coffee, hoping that the bitter brew will snap me back into focus.

As I make my way down the corridor toward the small break room, my steps quicken as I approach the door. The rush of adrenaline spikes through me, suffocating the worry that had been gnawing deep in my core. I can't shake the feeling of unease that pulls at the edges of my sanity, like a thin thread that's about to snap under pressure.

I push the break room door open and step inside, greeted by the familiar scent of freshly brewed coffee mingling with the stale aroma of the pastries left over from the morning break. Two of my colleagues are present, engaged in idle chatter as they pour their cups. I nod at them, trying to project normalcy, the façade of the unbothered officer who's in control—just as they expect me to be.

I reach for the coffee pot, pouring a cup, my hands trembling slightly as I clank the mug against the counter.

"Easy there, Captain," one of my colleagues jokes, glancing over at me. "You look like you've seen a ghost."

Awkward laughter erupts, but I don't join in. I swallow hard, ignoring the anxious twist in my stomach. Behind the humor lies an unease, an awareness of the storm brewing within me that others aren't privy to. I turn away, not wanting their probing eyes on me any longer.

"Just tired," I manage to say. I down the coffee in a single gulp before thinking better of it. It burns my throat, but what do I care? The heat forces me to focus on something, anything, outside myself.

I lean against the counter. Hints of anger bubble beneath my skin, restless and electric.

What if I lash out at someone here like I did at home?

I finish my cup quickly, the bitter taste lingering on my tongue. I set it down with more force than necessary. The noise echoes in the small room, and I see my colleague glance toward me again, worry flaring in her eyes.

Damn it. I need to get a grip.

I step forward just as the door swings open again. It's

General Benedict. My anxiety spikes. He offers a casual wave, oblivious to the tempest brewing within me.

"Teague! Got a sec?" He walks in, hands tucked into his pockets, and I can't quite decipher whether he's expecting an easy-going conversation or something more serious in nature.

"Sure," I reply, trying to sound more collected than I feel.

"Just wanted to check in on you. Dr. Mallory contacted me again," he starts, his voice easy but his expression intense. "She seems worried. Genuinely so."

The words slice through me, each one stirring something volatile that I'm desperate to contain. The betrayal in her speaking to him again gnaws at my insides.

Does she not realize how serious it is to approach my commanding officer—not once, but twice? How could she not keep this between us?

"Was she here?"

"She called."

"I'm dealing with it," I say curtly, trying to extricate myself from the conversation. I can't afford to let my emotions spill over.

Not here. Not now.

Benedict doesn't miss a beat. "How? By smashing furniture and pushing away the one person who cares about you? That's not going to work for long."

His tone is firm, yet I detect a hint of sympathy in his eyes, and it only fuels my anger. The shade of judgment lingers—who does he think he is to step into my marriage?

"I appreciate your concern, but I really don't need help," I insist, my voice tight.

"I'm not talking about 'help' in the conventional sense," he replies, his eyes narrowing slightly. "I mean real help. You can't face these demons alone, Oscar. They're going to consume you from the inside out if you keep pretending everything is okay."

We hold each other's gaze, the tension in the small break room almost palpable. On one side, there's General Benedict, an authority figure urging me to confront the issues that twist and turn within me. On the other is the part of myself willing to bury everything deep, to keep the façade intact.

"Look, I used to see you as a solid officer. A reliable leader," the general continues, voice lowered. "Don't let this break you. It's not just about your career. It's about your life."

I resist the urge to dissect his words. He doesn't know what it's like, what I've been through. He doesn't understand the torment racing inside my skull.

"I said I'm fine," I manage to spit out, the weight of my denial heavy on my tongue.

"Fine? You're not fine," he presses. "Your wife is scared of what's happening to you. It sounds like she's becoming scared *of* you. You don't want that."

"Scared of me?" I scoff, but it's laced with venom. "I'm not the enemy here."

My voice rises involuntarily, and the tension crackles in the air, thick and charged. The anger that's been simmering explodes just beneath the surface, and as I glance at the coffee cup again, I'm overwhelmed by the urge to lash out. To prove I'm still in control.

"You share a home with her, a life. She has every reason to be worried when you can't even keep your punches controlled—"

"That's it. I'm done with this conversation," I growl, cutting him off, spinning around to face the counter again.

The coffee cup, now empty, is a monument to my rising frustration, and I find it hard to ignore the impulse to put something in its place. Something that breaks.

I feel Benedict step closer. The authoritative tone in his voice shifts. I could get into huge, life-altering trouble for acting this way in front of my commanding officer.

"Marine, you can't keep running from this," he says. "You're one step away from hurting someone. Maybe even yourself."

"Shut the hell up!" I bark in response, the heat surging through me with every syllable. The room tilts, the walls feeling like they're closing in. I find my hands fisting at my sides again.

"Don't raise your voice at me," he snaps back, his eyes flashing as he tries to hold his ground.

"Then don't speak to me like I'm a child. You don't know the first thing about my life." With a swift motion, I slam my fist down onto the counter, the noise echoing violently within the confines of the small kitchen space.

The sound reverberates mercilessly, an explosion of control shattering the fragile atmosphere. In the silence that follows, every gaze in the room shifts, startled by the outburst.

I'm beyond caring. The anger surges through my veins. "I'm not fragile, and I'm not broken," I howl, though the words feel hollow even as they escape my lips.

General Benedict retains a semblance of composure, but the flicker of concern in his eyes betrays his thoughts. "This isn't about strength. It's about recognizing that you need help. That pushing everyone away isn't the answer. It's never the answer."

His words barely register over the surge of violent

emotions. Each pulse of anger seems to build like a dam on the brink of collapse. I can feel the enormity of the shadows looming closer, threatening to snuff out everything.

I want to maintain my dignity and my composure, but the frustration surges once again. My muscles feel coiled and spring-loaded.

"You don't understand!" I shout. "There are things at play here beyond the surface. I'm being pulled in directions I can't control." My voice cracks at the end, frustration warring with desperation. "You think I'm putting on a show for you?"

Benedict steps back slightly, perhaps recognizing the perilous line he's treading. "I'm not suggesting that at all. But vacuuming everything inside isn't a solution. And ignoring your wife's fears will only make this worse."

"Worse? How could it get worse?" I snarl, my eyes blazing as I inch closer to him, words spilling hotly from my lips. A part of me knows it isn't just General Benedict who should bear the brunt of all this. "I could lose everything, and for what? For trying to be 'normal' when the world is swirling around me like it's gone mad?"

He opens his mouth as if to retort, but I see the thought die on his tongue as something trembles in the air—some new revelation looming, wrapped in tension.

And then it happens.

I reach a breaking point.

Without even consciously thinking about it, I shove the coffee pot off the counter, sending it crashing to the floor in a spray of glass and hot liquid. The shattering sound reverberates, drowning out everything else, echoing the chaos bursting to the surface inside me as if screaming for release.

A gasp escapes the general's lips, his eyes widening in

shock. The room falls deathly silent, every pair of eyes drawn to the disaster I just created.

"Damn it, Marine! What's wrong with you?" he curses, visibly shifting, now unsettled. "Are you really going to let it get to this point? Get your shit together, Captain Teague!"

That one phrase cuts deeper than any blade ever could.

"Get my shit together?" I retort as my vision narrows to a blurry red haze of anger. "You think you know me? You think you can fix this with condescension and orders? I'm not one of your new recruits. I'm a goddamn officer!"

The pulse of indignation thrums in my veins, feeding the storm brewing inside me. I can't control it anymore. I stride toward him, fists clenched, the remnants of the broken coffee pot littering the floor, sharp shards reflecting the light like pieces of my fraying sanity.

"Pull it back, Teague!" Carl commands, raising his hands in a placating manner. I can see his veneer of authority cracking, the way the color drains from his face as he realizes what I'm capable of.

"Why should I? What do you know?" I challenge, my voice a low growl.

The tension morphs into an electric silence—a standoff in the middle of a cramped break room. My heart races, primal instinct driving me to fight. In the periphery of my mind, though, I know I'm crossing a line, enough that waves of cold dread sweep through the fleeting rage.

In the next moment, the door swings open behind Benedict, and in steps a fellow officer—one of my peers—his eyes widening at the scene before him.

"What the hell is going on?" he asks, looking between us, confusion taking hold.

His presence snaps me back just a fraction, the clarity of the moment seeping into my muddled thoughts. I stand rigid, still predatory, adrenaline coursing through my body as I stride forward without thinking. The instinct to assert dominance overrides concern.

I should be the officer people look up to. The backbone of the team.

"Nothing you need to worry about, Matthews," I bark, and my voice comes out sharper, more controlled. I can feel the weight of the general's stare boring into the side of my neck, but I ignore it, focusing instead on maintaining a facade that means I'm still functional, still the man I'm supposed to be.

"Looks like everything's fine," Jeremy Matthews says with raised eyebrows, catching my tone. "But maybe step back and—"

"Like you said, everything's—" I start to retort, but the fear in the room becomes palpable, and Benedict glares at me, his expression a mix of disappointment and disbelief. It's an expression I recognize all too well. It's the same one I see in my own reflection.

"Shut it down, Teague," General Benedict warns, his voice low but commanding. "This isn't a battlefield, and you're not on some deployment. You need to think before you act."

All at once, the adrenaline that fueled my anger dissipates, leaving behind a chilling sense of emptiness. I'm aware that I've crossed a line—one that makes me seem less like a leader and more like a ticking time bomb.

I open my mouth to defend myself, but the words die before they can form. What can I say? That I'm losing control? That a part of me feels like it's slipping into a darkness so profound I can't bear to look?

The room feels smaller now, the glances from my colleagues—first Benedict and now Matthews—heavy with concern that I'm unable to shake. I dig my nails into my palms, willing myself to breathe.

After a beat of silence, I finally tear my gaze from Matthews. "I'm fine," I grunt, gripping the edge of the counter with white knuckles. "Just having a bad day."

Matthews doesn't look convinced, glancing at Carl for confirmation.

General Benedict's expression might as well be carved from stone. "We're done here. I'll fill out the necessary reports, but you'll be off the schedule until you get this sorted. Go home, Captain. Talk to your wife. Figure things out."

I stare at him, shock racing through me. "Off the schedule?" I echo, disbelief lacing my words. I've worked too damn hard to throw it all away now.

"Yeah, off the schedule," Carl reaffirms, his voice firm. "For your sake and everyone else's. We're worried about you."

"Worried?" I repeat flatly. "This is bullshit."

I clench my fists, fighting against the bloom of rage that stirs anew. But before I can lunge at Benedict or Matthews in my frustration, the general steps forward, his brow knitted in concern. "This isn't a punishment. It's a chance for you to take a step back, to breathe and reconsider where you want to go from here."

"And what if I don't want to?" I respond.

"You don't have a choice."

Chapter Eleven

SIERRA

I have a job interview today.

It's been a while since I've worked full time. Since before our wedding, in fact. I had decided to take some time off to get moved and settled in Virginia. When the helo crash happened and Oscar found himself facing a tough recovery, I pushed my search back indefinitely.

It's time, though. Getting out of the house and doing something to occupy my mind will be good for me. Good for *us*. Not to mention, I'll lose momentum in my career if I wait too long to continue building my resume and making professional connections.

It's sunny when I arrive at the Children's National Hospital in Fairfax. I pull into a parking spot and check my lipstick in the rearview mirror. I'm wearing another pencil skirt—red this time—with heels and a curve-hugging sweater. I decide to wear my reading glasses—not because I really need them to see, but because I think they make me look smart.

If I'm lucky, the good folks in this big, shiny building will select me to provide behavioral health services to kids in the

D.C. metro area. The psychologist interviewing me is another Emory alum. Maybe I'm naive, but I'm feeling positive about my chances of getting hired.

If I get the job, it will be approximately a 30-minute commute from home in Woodbridge, and that's if I can beat traffic. Oscar has roughly the same commute time to Quantico. Only he travels south from home and I'll be traveling north.

Maybe that's a good thing. A little distance during the work week could do us good.

The combination of the sunshine and the prospect of securing a job I'm proud of has me in good spirits.

It's almost enough to distract me from the troubles with my husband.

Almost.

As I step into the hospital's entrance, my heart flutters with a mix of excitement and nerves. I navigate my way to the designated waiting area, where the soft pastel colors and cheerful decorations bring a smile to my face. Children's laughter fills the air, a reminder of why I've chosen this path —to help those who need it most.

Beneath the excitement, though, lies an undercurrent of worry. Will today mark a turning point for us? Will I finally find the rhythm I've been missing in my life recently? Or will things somehow, inexplicably, unravel. My gut tells me it's the latter.

I push those thoughts aside, focusing instead on my interview.

After a brief wait, I'm ushered into a conference room where Dr. Sonal Singh is seated, a warm smile greeting me. Our conversation flows easily at first, rekindling memories of my time at Emory. I'm feeling confident, the tension in my shoulders easing as I discuss my professional experiences and aspirations. Dr. Singh is friendly. I'll bet she'd be an excellent boss to work for.

Just when I start to believe I'm truly making progress, the door swings open, and in walks Oscar.

He looks disheveled, as if he's just come from a battle instead of an office. The controlled persona he usually wears is now marred with tension. His eyes scan the room, landing on me, and for a moment, the air feels thick.

This doesn't make any sense.

"What are you doing here?" I ask, surprised.

My heart quickens as his expression darkens. I can see the undercurrents of anger rippling through him, a storm brewing just beneath the surface. I told him I was coming here for an interview, but I never imagined he'd come to find me.

"I came to check on you," he replies curtly, his gaze still locked on a spot over my shoulder. The way he's pointedly avoiding eye contact sends a ripple of unease through me.

Dr. Singh clears her throat. "Hello, Captain Teague, I presume? It's nice to see you in person," she says smoothly, attempting to ease the tension.

Oscar's jaw tightens, but he doesn't respond. Instead, his gaze drops from the doctor to me, narrowing. "I'd rather not wait to figure out why you chose to wear that," he snaps, his voice low but laced with frustration.

"What do you mean?" I murmur, suddenly feeling self-conscious as I glance down at my outfit.

It's professional, stylish even.

To Oscar's eyes, apparently, my choice of wardrobe is

something more insidious. How? He's never been concerned about what I've worn before.

He takes a step closer, and my heart falls as I realize that his agitation is escalating. "You don't think I noticed? This isn't a date, Sierra. You're here for a job interview, not to flaunt yourself."

Dr. Singh shifts in her seat, eyeing the pair of us with uncertainty. I can feel the room growing small. "Oscar, that's not fair," I say, my voice steady but laced with incredulity. "I dressed professionally. You know I want to make a good impression."

"A good impression? Or the wrong kind of impression?" He gestures to my fitted sweater, his frustration palpable in the space between us. Then, without warning, he slams a fist against the doorframe, startling both me and Dr. Singh. The noise reverberates in the small room.

"Stop!" my voice rises. I shoot a glare at Oscar. "You can't act like this. Not here."

"Why should I care?" he retaliates. "This is exactly the kind of behavior that makes it hard for me to concentrate on what's happening in my life, Sierra."

Dr. Singh shifts in her seat again, clearly uncomfortable and unsure how to intervene.

"This isn't okay, Oscar," I say, trying to keep my voice calm, though the fear in my chest is rising. "You need to control yourself."

He scoffs, an anger boiling up that makes my head spin. "And what? Pretend everything's fine? You think I'm going to play house while my mind is screaming at me?"

With each word, I can feel the situation spiraling further

out of control. This is not the Oscar I fell in love with. This is a man on the verge of breaking.

"Just leave. Please. You're ruining everything," I plead, hoping to cut through the chaos in his mind. "You're ruining my chance at a future—our future."

"Maybe that's the fucking point," he snaps back, his eyes burning with anger. "Maybe you need to realize you're not the only one who gets to make choices here."

The tension surging through the room feels electric, hot enough to set everything ablaze. Oscar's eyes flare with anger, and I feel my heart speed up in response. Every nerve in my body screams for calm, for normalcy, but the mounting storm cannot be contained.

"Where is he?" Oscar demands, a low growl lurking just beneath the surface of his words.

"He, who?" I ask.

"Who are you dressing to impress?"

"What are you talking about?" I snap back, torn between bewilderment and a rising tide of fear. "There's no one else here."

His fists clench at his sides, the tension radiating off him like heat from a furnace. "Oh, don't play innocent with me. I can see it. You think I don't know what you're doing? You think I can just stand by while you parade yourself around in front of other men?"

Dr. Singh shifts nervously in her chair, watching the two of us with wide eyes, her expression torn between concern and disbelief. I can feel every atom in the air grow thick with dread as her silent observation becomes a reminder that we're in a public space, and this is not how things should be.

"Oscar, this isn't about that. This is a job interview. I'm

trying to launch my career here in Virginia." I step forward, desperate to reach him through the haze of jealousy that has fogged his mind. "You're being ridiculous."

"And you think that tight sweater is going to help you? What do you think this is, some sort of fashion show? You know the kind of people around here," he shoots back, his voice rising. "What did you expect?"

Now he's insulting the people here? The accusation strikes me, and a wave of shock washes over me. I take a breath, forcing the anger to ebb just enough to regain my composure. I will not let this escalate further.

"Oscar, you're not being fair," I plead. "I've done nothing to warrant this reaction."

"Nothing? This whole place—" he gestures around the room as if it embodies some great sin "—it's filled with people who want to undermine me, and you're giving them ammunition."

"Am I?" I ask, my patience wearing thin. "Or are you just creating illusions in your mind? I'm here to better our lives, to help needy children and advance my career. Not to tear us apart. I love you, and I'm trying to make things work."

His gaze darkens, eyes narrowed, as though my words fuel a fire he can no longer control. "You think I don't know that?"

He takes a step forward, invading the space between us. "I don't need saving. I need you to see the truth—that I'm no longer who you thought I was."

As the words leave his mouth, the truth behind them hits me harder than any blow. I swallow, something sharp and cold settling in my stomach.

"I'm trying to help you!" I exclaim, voice wavering slightly as I hold my ground. "You can't act like this and expect me to just fix everything behind the scenes."

The fire in his eyes morphs into something akin to fear—a deep, unnerving dread that encompasses everything. "I'm not the only one who might be lying to you!" He calls out, the accusation striking like a bolt of lightning. It doesn't make a bit of sense.

I open my mouth to respond, but pain constricts my throat. "Oscar, what are you talking about?"

He isn't listening. His mind is spinning in his own net of paranoia as he paces the floor.

"This is why I can't stay," he says. "You don't even understand the chaos. They've done something to me, and I'm not the only pawn on their board. I can't go to Djibouti either, though. That could be career suicide. I don't know—"

"Calm down," I plead, trying to reach for him and connect, but he pulls away, the fear morphing into an even more desperate anger as he raises his voice.

I had no idea there was a possibility of him going to Djibouti. The prospect sounds like a relief of sorts, but it also terrifies me.

"Do I scare you, Sierra? Am I just some joke to you?"

"No, Oscar!" I shout, my heart racing. "You're not."

I glance at Dr. Singh and see that she's grown very uncomfortable. She picks up a phone on her desk and pushes a few buttons. She's calling security, no doubt.

I don't blame her.

Within seconds, the door bursts open, and two security officers step inside. Their presence is towering, but their faces reveal uncertainty about what they've walked into. I can see the tension in Oscar rise again, igniting his anger like a match to gasoline.

"Oscar, don't!" I call out, urgency coloring my voice, as he lunges for a nearby stack of files, tossing them into the air like confetti.

Papers scatter, floating down in disarray, and I watch as the clarity of professionalism disintegrates before my eyes.

"Oscar!" I scream, desperation tinging my tone, but he's not looking at me anymore. He's lost in his own whirlwind of chaos, the world around him blurring into shades of red.

One of the security officers tries to approach him, hands raised in a calming gesture, but it's futile. "Sir, you need to calm down. We're here to help."

Help? To Oscar, those words only add fuel to the fire. I've learned that much the hard way.

"Help?" he snarls, turning rapidly to confront them, his expression wild, fists clenched tightly, body coiled with tension. "You think this is about help? Maybe you're the reason this is all happening."

He turns to me, eyes blazing. "Everyone thinks they can just poke around in my life, my marriage, and tell me how to feel. This is none of your fucking business!"

"No!" I reply, furious now. "This is about you, Oscar—your behavior. You can't act like this."

The second officer steps forward cautiously, realizing the situation is dangerously volatile. "Sir, if you don't get control of yourself, we're going to have to restrain you. Please, lower your voice and think about what you're doing."

That only seems to escalate Oscar further, and in a fit of rage, his arm swings out, knocking the security officer aside. "Get away from me!" he yells, the echoes of his voice crashing against the walls of Dr. Singh's tranquil office like thunder.

My pulse pounds as I realize the gravity of the situation, instinctively stepping closer to the officers. "You don't understand!" I shout. "He's not himself. He's never been like this before. Something's wrong."

The officers exchange glances, assessing the situation, while Oscar's paranoia reaches a fever pitch. He swings again, this time knocking a heavy metal chair across the room. It collides with the wall, creating a resonating bang that sends shockwaves through all of us.

"Stop!"

I cry out, but my voice is drowned in the crisis. As the chair careens toward me, I attempt to step back, but the momentum is too fast, too sudden. The chair clips my leg, sending pain sparking through my body. I stumble, landing hard against the edge of the desk, the air rushing from my lungs in a gasp.

"Oscar!" I shout, the furious blend of pain and panic amplifying my voice.

In that instant, the fury etched across his face dissolves into horror as he realizes what he's done. He rushes toward me, concern slicing through the anger that had consumed him just moments before. "Sierra! Oh God, I didn't—"

I wince as I push myself up, the sharp ache in my leg radiating upwards, but I shake my head dismissively. "I'm fine."

I'm not fine, but I need him to see that I'm trying to be strong. I don't want him to spiral further into despair or blame. His hands hover uncertainly over my shoulder, not quite resting there, as if he fears breaking something that was already so fragile.

"Did it hurt?" he asks, his voice shaking as he crouches before me, eyes wide and glistening with anguish. "I am so, so sorry."

"It's just a bruise," I say quickly, trying to deflect the panic shadowing his features. "It's not a big deal, really."

The officers, witnessing the chaos unfold, are quick to step in. "Sir, you need to step back," one of them instructs, now more assertive in the face of the escalating situation.

"No, I can handle this," Oscar insists, defensive.

"You need to take a step back for your own safety as well as hers," the second officer says firmly, maintaining professional distance as they steadily position themselves beside me.

"I'm not a threat!" my husband snaps, the frustration boiling over again. Real foam and fury seem to be spilling from his lips. "You don't know what I've been through. I can take care of my—"

"I said I'm fine." I interject sharply, the words coming out louder than I intended. I stand, smoothing the front of my skirt. "Dr. Singh, Officers, I apologize for the disruption. My husband will take care of me at home."

Chapter Twelve

OSCAR

I latch onto Sierra's words, hearing the urgency in her tone. My stomach churns with a mix of anxiety and regret, knowing I've crossed a line I never intended to.

When I see her attempt to steady herself, I feel something spark within me—a desperate need to fix what I've broken.

"Yes, let's go home. I'm sorry for all of this," I murmur, my grip on her arm softening as we inch toward the door. The officers watch, their faces concerned but filled with a hesitant understanding. They know that I'm not myself. I'm grateful they're letting this end quietly.

Once inside my car, I drive in silence, my hands clenched tightly around the steering wheel as my thoughts race. Sierra follows me in her car, and I'm glad for the hour-long drive home to collect my thoughts before I speak to her again. I barely hear the familiar streets of Woodbridge roll by. The images of what just happened, the chaos, and the anger flash across my mind like some war-torn battlefield I can't escape. All that matters now is that I don't make this any worse. Not for her, and not for me.

When we arrive at our house, I notice how quiet it feels. The air is still, as if the very walls are holding their breath, waiting to see if I can somehow mend what I've shattered.

"I'll make us something to eat," I say as I step inside, eager for a distraction. The simple act of cooking has always felt grounding, and right now, I need anything that can help stabilize my mind.

Sierra moves into the living room, her footsteps soft against the hardwood floor. I can hear her shifting things around, though her movements seem hesitant and indecisive.

Stepping into the kitchen, I take a deep breath, allowing the familiar scents of garlic and herbs to invade my senses. I can almost picture us, seated at the table—laughter spilling over plates, a glass of wine in hand.

But today isn't that day.

As I chop vegetables, my mind drifts back to the gentle rhythm of our lives before the crash—lazy Sundays spent in bed, spontaneous adventures, and late-night talks under the stars. I pick up a photo frame that had been tucked away on the counter. It's one of our wedding pictures—the moment we exchanged vows. I remember how joyous we both felt that day, two souls interwoven, each promising to stand by the other no matter what the world threw at us.

"A beautiful beginning," I had said then, my voice filled with emotion. It was more than I had ever hoped for.

Now, here I am in the kitchen of what is supposed to be our happy home, and I can hardly recognize the broken man I've become.

Sierra enters, leaning against the doorway, her presence both comforting and heavy with concern. "You okay?" she asks softly.

I nod, even though I want to scream that I'm anything but okay. "Just cooking. Thought it might help."

"Smells good," she replies, attempting to meet my gaze, but I can see the worry etched in her expression.

"Yeah, not like it used to," I say lightly, trying to poke fun at myself, but the words come out sharper than I intended.

"I didn't mean—" she starts, but I cut her off, my frustration bubbling close to the surface.

"Can we just drop it?" I snap, the tension hanging heavy and taut in the kitchen air. I can feel her flinch at my tone, and guilt washes over me at her reaction.

The silence stretches on, an ache pulsing between us, but I can't bring myself to apologize. Somehow, I fear that it will make it worse.

In a bid to change the subject, I continue preparing dinner. The rhythm of chopping vegetables becomes my refuge, slicing through the tension. Secretly, I wish things would just go back to how they were. If only I could crawl out of this pit of darkness.

"Let's eat outside," Sierra suggests, her voice barely above a whisper. "The weather looks nice. It's cool, but sunny."

The idea is appealing, and I nod in agreement. "Sure. I'll grab the place settings."

We follow the path we've walked hundreds of times across the yard, back to the small patio where we set up a rickety wooden table and mismatched chairs.

As I set the table, I can feel the weight of her gaze.

"Oscar," she finally says, tension coiling within me even before she continues. "I need to know if you're really going to try and make this work. I can't live this way."

I pause, her words settling into the pit of my stomach like

a stone. I want to tell her yes, that I'm committed to making things better, to finding a way to fix what's broken. I've already said as much. But the truth is wrapped in shadows, and I fear that trying to shed light on it will only hurt her more.

"I'm trying," I say, the words feeling inadequate even as they leave my lips. "I really am. I just—" I take a breath, searching for the right way to express the turmoil inside me. "I don't even fully understand what I'm trying to fix."

Sierra nods slowly, her expression softening, but the flicker of uncertainty in her eyes only adds to the tension. "I get that," she replies gently. "But it feels like you're retreating further and further into yourself."

A discomfort seeps through me as I lean against the weathered patio table. "It's hard to share what's happening up here," I admit, tapping my temple. Frustration begins to build again. "You think I want to feel like this? I can't just flip a switch and change it."

"I know," she says, and I can see the flicker of hurt distressing her features. "Let's talk about something else."

"All right, let's change the subject," I say, taking a deep breath, letting my frustration ebb just a little. "How's your leg feeling?"

I don't want to dwell on what happened, but I need to know she's okay.

"It's just a bruise," she replies, her voice light, though I can see the shadow of concern still clouding her eyes. "Nothing to worry about. You really didn't mean to hurt me."

I lean across the table, closing the distance between us

once more. "Still, I'm sorry. That's not who I am. I don't want to be that person."

Her smile is small, almost fragile, but it's there. "You're still my Oscar."

I want to say something, to promise her that I will find a way to break free from this, but the words stick in my throat. Instead, I reach for her hand, intertwining our fingers.

"Why don't we do something special tonight?" I propose, trying to give us a distraction from the seriousness of our reality. "Just us. Maybe a movie? Some time spent relaxing together?"

Her eyes flicker with a hint of surprise, then warmth. "That sounds nice," she replies. "We could really use that."

"Good. I want to remind you of the other side of me—the side you fell in love with," I say, my stomach knotting at the thought. "The side that isn't filled with this noise."

"Just promise me you'll be calm," she replies earnestly.

I nod, leaning closer, determined to show her I can be that man—even if it's just for a fleeting moment. "I promise."

As the meal winds down, I glance around the yard—our yard. Sunlight streams through the trees, casting patches of light that dance across the grass. Memories flood over me, the days we spent here planning our lives together, the laughter and joy that once echoed within these walls. I want to reclaim that, to immerse myself in that love again.

"Let's have a little fun," I suggest, my tone shifting to something more playful. I inch closer, keeping my gaze locked on her. "How about we make dessert together? You can pick the recipe, and I'll do my best to help or ... maybe we can indulge in some spontaneous experimentation?"

She chuckles softly, her eyes brightening as she considers

the idea. "What are we experimenting with? My Grandmother Mallory was a baker, but I don't remember much of what she taught me. That was a long time ago."

"I'm ready for anything," I reply, feeling a sense of determination washing over me. "Besides, I trust your instincts."

With that, I lean in, playfully brushing my lips against hers, feeling her warmth surge through me like the sun breaking through clouds. "Just one kiss for good luck," I whisper against her lips, my cheeks turning slightly pink as I pull back, unable to mask the grin that spreads across my face.

She rises to the challenge, and I feel a flutter of excitement as she leans forward this time, catching me by surprise. Her kiss is soft and tender, but it also ignites a fire that spreads from my chest to the tips of my fingers. I want to pull her close again, to drown out every doubt.

"We should do more of that," she murmurs against my lips, and the suggestion strikes hard. "More romance, less turmoil."

"Yes," I reply, my heart racing. "Let's focus on rebuilding our connection. I need that, Sierra."

As we pull apart, she gets to her feet, a glimmer of determination etched in her features. I rise to join her.

"First," I say, trying to mirror her energy. "Let's pick something outrageous for dessert. It should be fun. You know, put our culinary skills to the test."

Her laughter rings out, and the sound feels like music to my ears. "Okay! Challenge accepted! How about we make chocolate soufflé? I've always wanted to try it."

"It has a reputation for being difficult, but I hear it's all about timing and careful folding of the egg whites," I say.

"Perfect, then we'll start with that," she replies, her excitement palpable. We go inside and I watch as she moves around the kitchen, already diving into the recipe that she found on her phone. There's a spark returning to her eyes, and it fills me with hope.

As she gathers the ingredients, I step closer, wrapping my arms around her waist from behind. "You know," I murmur, my breath tickling her ear, "I never thought I'd find someone who could make soufflé look so sexy."

She laughs softly, leaning back against me for a moment before gracefully breaking free and pivoting to face me, a playful glint sparkling in her eyes. "Well, I believe that's my secret weapon—you see, I'm all about finessing my way through tough challenges."

I chuckle, leaning against the counter. "How about I be your sous-chef? You know, just in case it collapses, we can pretend it was my fault."

"Good idea," she says. "But if we end up in that situation, I'll need to keep you busy while I whip up a new batch. You might need to distract me. Like you did at the Marine Corps Ball last November. Do you remember that?"

Her laughter dances through the air, and I can't help but feel lighter.

"Absolutely. That distraction led us to a coat closet, if my memory serves me. Consider me your distraction, then," I say, smirking while reaching out to stroke her cheek gently. "But if we're doing this together, I need to know your baking skills are as good as your ... *other* skills. Show me what you've got, Ms. Mallory."

Her breath hitches slightly as she looks me in the eyes. "Careful, Captain. I just might impress you."

I step even closer, lowering my voice as I lean in, letting

my lips hover just above hers. "I have no doubt you'll blow me away. But if things go awry, I expect you to blame yourself entirely. Your secret's safe with me. I might even help you hide the evidence."

Her gaze flickers with mischief, and she bites her lip, unable to suppress a teasing smile.

Before we can start on the dessert, we fall into each other's arms. Passionate kisses lead to a heated embrace, enveloping us in a cocoon of warmth. Each touch rekindles the connection we've been fighting to regain.

"I think we should have a dessert before the dessert," I suggest playfully, backing her against the counter. Her laughter is like a balm to my soul. For all the storms brewing inside my head, this moment feels tangible. This is something I can hold onto.

"Now who's being ridiculous?" she teases, but the playful light in her eyes tells me she's more than willing to indulge. "We haven't even made the soufflé yet."

"Exactly. We can't be distracted by baking when such vital pre-soufflé activities are on the table," I reply, my voice low and suggestive as I lean closer, brushing my lips against hers once more, feeling her breathe in the moment.

Our kisses deepen, the world around us fading into the background. My hands find themselves weaving through her hair, holding her closer as if to siphon every ounce of connection we have left. It's primal, raw—a hunger that we both seem to share.

"I can't remember the last time we just enjoyed each other's company like this," Sierra breathes, her lips brushing mine, barely a whisper. "I mean, the other night was nice, but it didn't ..."

She trails off, and I appreciate her not mentioning the splintered bedside table. I'd rather forget that it happened.

"Neither can I," I admit, pulling back just enough to gaze into her eyes. "We've been through so much, but I still want to share life with you. I want us to thrive, not just survive. I'm so sorry I lost my temper today. I'm so sorry your leg got hurt—"

"Shh, then let's savor this," she murmurs, that wonderful smile returning. "And let's create something delicious, even if it's just for a moment."

I guide her back toward the open kitchen, a renewed energy invigorating our steps as I reach for the ingredients laid out on the counter. We catch glimpses of the old rhythm we once shared, moving fluidly, almost instinctively, side by side as we gather flour, chocolate, and eggs.

"This is a delicate process," I say, trying to sound overly serious as I pull off my sweater and toss it onto a chair. "I'm fully committed to rapid-fire soufflé rescue operations, should the need arise."

"That's the spirit," she replies, eyes sparkling with warmth.

The rich scent of melting chocolate wafts through the air, intoxicating and delicious. As we stir the batter together, I lean in, brushing my lips against her neck. "I can't help but think this is more than just baking," I murmur.

She glances up at me, her eyes full of mischief. "You mean chocolate can save our marriage?"

"Stranger things have happened," I reply, grinning as I pull her closer. There's a moment of hesitation where time stretches, both of us aware of how pivotal it is.

It's not just about the soufflé.

Sierra bites her lip, that spark of fear and excitement flickering in her gaze. "Okay, Captain. Let's make this work."

Encouraged, I deepen the kiss, pouring every ounce of love and hope into the gesture. Everything else fades away.

We allow ourselves to get lost in each other, shutting out the world outside. When our bodies connect once more, it feels like a statement reaffirming that we are still here.

Still fighting. Still holding on.

As the evening unfolds and I make love to my wife, we know the journey ahead won't be easy, but for tonight, it's enough.

PART TWO
Predatory Instincts

Chapter Thirteen

SIERRA

Four Days Later
The Fateful Day

It's Friday, and Oscar has gone to work to beg Carl for another chance. After spending a few days becoming increasingly agitated, I encouraged him to approach the Marine Corps one more time. I'm home alone, showered and dressed to go somewhere, though I have no idea where.

What I didn't say in front of everyone in Dr. Singh's office the other day is that a realization settled over me when the chair struck my leg. It hit me like a bolt of lightning. I know, like I know my own name, that I'm in danger. Just because Oscar wasn't throwing anything directly at me, doesn't mean that he won't. It's only a matter of time before he turns his anger on me.

I'm terrified.

Sure, I made love to him and played nice. I did it again last night, too. What was I supposed to do? If I act scared, it will just be a sign of weakness. That won't end well for me.

Besides, I've got to convince someone that Oscar isn't himself. That will only happen if we present a united front. I've got to get my husband help—real help—before it's too late.

I'm pacing the living room, the tension in my body tightening with each step. The walls feel like they're closing in around me, and every creak of the floorboard echoes my mounting anxiety.

My phone buzzes on the table, momentarily distracting me from the spiral of thoughts consuming my mind. I check the screen and see Dr. Singh's name flash across it. She's called around this time each day for the past few days, but I haven't had the courage to pick up.

Taking a deep breath, I answer, forcing myself to maintain a calm exterior. "Hello?"

"Hi, Sierra! It's Sonal Singh. I wanted to check in on you after the events that took place in my office," she says, her tone professional yet warm.

"Hi, Dr. Singh. I'm doing okay. Just trying to sort things out," I reply. I deliberate how much to share.

"I understand how overwhelming everything must be right now," she says. "It's not uncommon to feel a surge of fear in situations like this. I encourage you to take care of yourself. If you ever feel unsafe, I urge you to consider staying at a shelter for a little while, even if just temporarily."

Her words shake me. I hadn't thought about a shelter. The very idea of leaving our home, my safe space, sends a wave of dread cascading through me. If I can just get Oscar the help he needs, everything will be okay. He isn't a bad guy.

"No, that won't be necessary," I respond quickly. Maybe too quickly. "Oscar hasn't hurt me. We had a ... misunderstanding, I guess. I just need to give him some space. I'm sure he'll be fine."

I'm not sure if I'm trying to convince her, or myself.

"Misunderstanding," she repeats thoughtfully. "That's one way to look at it, but it's important to focus on the language surrounding what happened. Those kinds of outbursts are significant. Please keep in mind that when people lose control, it can escalate quickly."

"I appreciate your concerns," I say. "I know it sounds serious, but I'm handling this. I promise."

"I would just hate to see you in a situation that could worsen, especially since you mentioned that Oscar's behavior has changed dramatically. If you need help, I want you to know that there are resources available to you. Please don't hesitate to reach out."

A knot forms in my stomach as I realize Dr. Singh is more aware of the potential ramifications of Oscar's behavior than I am. Suddenly, the gravity of my situation pulls me under, but I fight it.

"I'm okay, really," I say. "I appreciate the call and your concern."

I don't ask if I'm still a candidate for the job. I know I'm not. How could I be, after what happened?

I hang up the phone feeling slightly unsettled, Dr. Singh's words still ringing in my ears. Instead of succumbing to panic, I decide to reach out to Beth.

I scroll through my contacts and dial her number. I tap my index finger against the phone as I wait, hoping she'll answer. After a few rings, she picks up.

"Sierra! Is everything okay? You seemed a little off last Friday. I've wanted to call, but I didn't want to pry."

I take a breath, trying to steady my voice. "Hey, Beth. I was wondering if you wanted to grab lunch? I could really use a friend today."

"Of course! I'd love to," she replies, her enthusiasm seeping through the phone. "What time and where?"

"How about noon? We can hit that café near the bookstore in downtown Woodbridge?"

"Perfect! I'll see you there!"

As I hang up, a part of me relaxes, feeling the simplicity of reaching out to someone who knows me well. Details of recent events ruminate in my head, and I can't shake the unease that has taken root since Oscar's behavior shifted so dramatically.

After picking out a comfortable outfit—something cute but not too flashy—I grab my things and glance at the clock. I'm still a bit early, but maybe it's better that way. I can take a moment to breathe. To gather my thoughts before diving into whatever I need to share with Beth.

The drive to the café is calming, the familiar roads providing a semblance of normalcy. I park and step into the light perfume of fresh coffee and baked pastries as I enter the café. It's a cozy little spot filled with eclectic decor and the sounds of soft chatter.

I spot Beth seated at a corner table, beaming up at me as I approach. She's even earlier than I am. "Hey, you!" she says, pulling me into an enthusiastic hug.

"Hey! Thanks for meeting me," I reply, sinking into a chair across from her. She looks vibrant as ever, her smile infectious.

"Always for you. So tell me, how's the husband?" she asks,

her tone casual, but I can sense an undercurrent of concern and genuine interest.

She knows why we're here today.

I hesitate, muscles tightening as I think over how to express the turmoil threatening to splinter my increasingly fragile marriage. "Um, it's complicated," I start, unsure of the words as they fall from my mouth. "He's really struggling with some things since the helicopter crash."

Beth nods, and I can see her eyes carefully assessing the situation, the gears in her mind turning as she processes what I'm unfolding.

"I remember you mentioning how hard the adjustment must be after such a traumatic experience," she replies, her voice laced with empathy. "But what does that mean for you? Are you okay?"

I take a deep breath, the urge to confide rising as the familiar feeling of impending despair clings to the edges of my thoughts. "Honestly? Some days, it feels like I'm losing him. He's not the man I married. He's angry, restless, and he lashes out at inanimate objects like he's fighting demons I can't even see."

Beth's expression dims, her concern intensifying. "That sounds really serious, Sierra. Have you talked to him about it? Like, really talked?"

"I have," I reply, swallowing hard as I remember the frantic conversations, me trying to reach through the barriers he's begun to build between us. "I want to help him, but every time I push for answers, he shuts down. It's like there's a darkness looming over him that I can't penetrate."

She leans forward, her focus unwavering. "That's terrifying. Are you sure you're safe?"

"Safe?" I echo, my heart skimming a hard beat against my chest. "What do you mean?"

"What I mean is, if he's breaking things or showing violent tendencies, you need to get out. You're worth it. Your safety matters."

"I appreciate your concern, but he wouldn't hurt me. It's not like that," I insist, though a note of doubt laces my voice.

I have doubts—real concerns—but the thought of leaving him still feels unbearable. Oscar is still my husband. I'm focused on figuring out a way to help him. A way to bring back the old Oscar I knew and loved.

"But if his anger is escalating, it may become a pattern," Beth urges softly, and I can see the genuine fear behind her eyes. "It's easy to downplay it, especially when we hope for change, but it's serious, Sierra. You can't ignore your instincts."

I nod slowly, but her words burrow deeper into my core. "I know you're right, but leaving feels impossible. I don't want to abandon him. I want to understand what's happening."

With a sigh, she leans back in her chair, crossing her arms. "Okay, let's take baby steps. What will you do if it escalates?"

The question rings in my mind—something I hadn't wanted to confront. The reality is heavy, weighing on my heart like a stone. "I don't know," I admit, my voice trembling slightly. "But I can't let it reach that point. I won't."

There's an unyielding determination in my words, though the cracks in my resolve are starting to show. I want to be strong—for Oscar, for us—but the truth is, I'm frightened of what he's becoming, of what chaos might ensue if this pattern continues unchecked.

"Acknowledge your fears," Beth presses gently. "You're not alone in this. You've already recognized there's something wrong. That's a huge step. Don't let fear of judgment or guilt keep you from seeing it clearly."

Her words resonate within me, stirring the embers of worries I've been trying to bury. I glance down at my tea, swirling the liquid as I contemplate the gravity of our conversation. If I'm honest with myself, I'm scared of losing Oscar to the darkness and scared of what he might do in that state.

"Maybe I should reach out to someone—like Dr. Singh," I say hesitantly, clutching at the idea like a lifeline. "She's the psychologist I interviewed with on Monday. A fellow Emory alum. I don't know what else to do."

"Absolutely," Beth agrees, her voice steady. "Talking to someone unbiased could provide you the ground you need to stand on. Their insight might shed light on what's really happening. And if Oscar ever does cross a line, you need an escape plan."

An escape plan.

The words echo in my mind. It feels extreme, almost irrational. But as I look into Beth's eyes, I see the truth reflected back. I've already witnessed the unraveling, and what happened with the nightstand could be just the tip of the iceberg.

"I'll call Dr. Singh back," I reply, the resolution building within me. "She actually called to check on me this morning."

"Oh? What happened at the interview?" Beth asks.

Reluctantly, I tell her everything. It's embarrassing to say, and my cheeks feel flush as I relay the story. I tell her about talking to Oscar's commanding officer, the splintered nightstand, and the scene at the children's hospital. Beth listens quietly, even as a perky young waitress brings our sandwiches and we eat.

Beth is a good, true friend. I'm glad I have her in my life. At least, she isn't telling me that everything is fine and will be okay.

It isn't fine, and it might not be okay.

"I hope Oscar finds his way back," I continue. "I can't have known him and simply walk away. It's just not who I am."

"I get that," Beth says softly. "And frankly, it's brave. But I don't want him to hurt you. Norman never would have—"

I cut her off before she can go there.

"I'll be careful," I reply, though the words feel almost insufficient.

We finish our lunch in thoughtful silence, each of us wrapped in our own contemplation of the uncertainties that lie ahead.

"What are you going to do next?" she asks. "It seems to me you should report this to someone. You know, document it. In case—"

I had toyed with the idea of going back to Quantico to talk to Carl again. Oscar seems to think the Marine Corps may be responsible for what's happening to him. Whether they are or not, as his commanding officer, Carl should step in.

"I think I'll go back to base and talk to General Benedict again," I say.

"Good," Beth says as we stand and she hugs me goodbye. "I'm going to stop by your house to check on you this evening, and I won't take no for an answer."

I nod appreciatively. "Thank you, Beth. For everything."

Chapter Fourteen

OSCAR

The day drags on like an anchor weighing me down as I drive toward Quantico.

Ever since we left the children's hospital a few days ago, I've been replaying the looks of concern on Sierra's face and the apprehension in Dr. Singh's eyes. Each moment spirals, and I can feel the threads of my once-stable existence unraveling faster than I can stitch them back together.

General Benedict calls while I'm less than a mile from base, his tone carefully neutral. There's no need for pleasantries. I already know what's coming.

“Captain Teague," he says, "the decision has been made. We need to keep you off the schedule until we can determine what's going on with you. Your safety and the safety of your fellow Marines is the priority.”

“Excuse me?” My voice tightens, disbelief and frustration surging through me. “You can't be serious. I'm fine to work. The incident was an isolated event, and I'm telling you I can handle my responsibilities. I need to get back in the field. In fact, I'm heading to base right now. I want to talk about deployment to Djibouti."

"We discussed this," Carl says firmly. "I'm not comfortable having you return until we can be certain you're fit for duty. I've instructed the military police officers to temporarily revoke your gate pass. It's not just about you. It's about the team."

"Is that right?" I retort, my pulse quickening. "And what gives you the authority to decide that? You don't know me like I thought you did."

I realize how ludicrous I sound. As my commanding officer, the general has the authority to do this ... and much more. Hell, at his rank, he could do it even if he wasn't my commanding officer.

Carl's voice turns cold and steady. "This isn't a discussion, Teague. It's for your own good," he says, but all I can hear is judgment.

The frustration roils inside me, igniting a toxic blend of anger and resentment, and I grip the phone tightly enough that a pang of pain jolts through my palm. "This is bullshit. You think keeping me off-base is the answer?"

"It's temporary. Until you get the help you need."

"Help?" I bark. I'm so damn sick of hearing that word. "I don't need help. I need to get back to work. You don't understand the kind of pressures I'm under."

"You're right. I don't understand everything, but I do know what seeing a doctor can do for you. Go see someone. That's an order. If this behavior continues—"

"Enough!" I shout, slamming the phone down onto the console in my car. The impact sends reverberations through the vehicle. The sound is satisfying, even as regret coaxes at the edges of my thoughts.

I toss the remnants of the call aside, the anger surging back as I drive into the base parking lot, outside of the gate. My hands grip the steering wheel with a vice-like hold, knuckles turning white. The world around me becomes a blur of shapes and sounds that I can't fully process, my mind spiraling deeper into the chaotic thoughts swirling inside.

As I step out of the car, I begin to pace back and forth, my breath quickening as the sensation of losing control creeps back in.

"I can't believe this," I mutter to myself, frustration bubbling over.

The thought of being sent away from the one thing I've dedicated my life to—the military and my fellow Marines—is like a condescending slap to the face.

I see other Marines driving past, their gazes flickering to me, and I feel a rush of heat flush my cheeks. I refuse to show them weakness. I'm Oscar Teague, a captain. They should respect me. They should see strength, not whatever this is.

Suddenly, my gaze lands on a stack of empty crates near the guard building, discarded from some recent supply delivery. One of them is tipped over, and instinctively, I kick it hard, sending it crashing against the brick wall. The noise echoes across the lot, and I can feel a few eyes turn my way, but I don't care.

I'm beyond caring.

"Get a grip, Teague!" I hiss to myself, shaking my head as I attempt to brush off the heat of embarrassment flooding my face.

As I start walking towards the entrance of the building, I

spot two privates standing off to the side, whispering while they glance in my direction. The sight of it ignites something deeper—a mix of rage and humiliation that surges through my veins.

"What the hell are you looking at?" I snap, my voice dripping with venom.

They jump, startled by my approach, and I see the confusion flash across their faces. The bravado I feel only fuels the fire, and before I can stop myself, I square my shoulders and step toward them.

"Do you have a problem, Private?" I growl, tension coiling in every muscle.

"Uh, no, sir! Just ... um, talking," one of them stammers, eyes wide.

"Talking? I don't want to hear you talking about me. This Corps runs on respect—you understand?"

"Yes, sir!" they both say in unison, their voices lifting in alarm as they instinctively straighten up.

I can see them flinch, and the sight stirs something within me, a sense of power that both unnerves and invigorates. It's a fragile thing. I can feel the edge of madness lurking just beneath the surface.

"Then keep your mouths shut," I bark, stepping back, the movement inadvertently sending a nearby trash can toppling to the ground with a loud clang. The sound echoes through the parking lot, louder than I anticipated, and a few heads turn to watch.

I'm losing it, but in that moment, I don't care. The pressure inside me is unbearable, a dam waiting to burst. As I stride away from the two privates, the reality of my situation spirals deeper into chaos. I can't keep doing this. Not while I feel like I'm on the brink of losing everything.

I get back in my car and head toward the gas station just outside the base, fueled by a mix of fury and an incoherent desire to drown the noise racing through my mind. I don't want to think about what I've done or what I might become. All I want is to escape.

I park and get out, looking for trouble.

As I step into the station, the bell jingles, a sharp reminder of normalcy that feels veiled behind my own turmoil. I move to the back where they stock their drinks, grabbing a bottle of water, my fingers trembling slightly as I twist the cap open.

Before I can take a sip, a man enters the store—a guy probably younger than I am, wearing a cocky grin and a military-style jacket that reeks of arrogance. He glances over at me, disdain clouding his gaze.

"Hey, Captain! Can't handle your troops out there?" he sneers, barely masking his amusement.

I don't recognize him, but he must recognize me. The taunt cuts deep.

"What did you say?" I demand, turning to face him fully, unable to keep my anger at bay.

"I said," he retorts, now approaching with a swagger, "you look like you're in over your head. Maybe some time away from the Marine Corps would help? Not everyone can cut it."

I feel the heat crawl up my neck, flooding my cheeks with anger. This punk doesn't know a thing about what I'm dealing with.

"You think you know how to handle this?" I say, my voice

steady but laced with rage. “Why don’t you step outside, and I’ll show you what it means to be a Marine?”

He raises an eyebrow, the mock amusement still plastered on his face as he steps closer, a twist of a smirk playing on his lips. “Oh, what’s the matter, Captain? Afraid your little tantrums will get you in trouble with the brass?”

The taunts fuel my anger, igniting something primal in me that I can’t suppress. "You have no idea what you're talking about," I growl, my fists clenching at my sides.

A few bystanders glance in our direction, sensing the brewing conflict. I can hear the low murmur of conversations hushed as they begin to pay attention.

“Maybe you should take your anger out on someone who cares,” he sneers, glancing at the cans lining the shelves, then back at me. "Oh wait. You already do that."

“You think you can just waltz in here and disrespect me? You think this is a game?” I step closer, matching his swagger with my own intensity, my heart pounding in my chest.

“Game? No, I’m just here to watch you crash and burn.” He chuckles, leaning against the cooler as if he knows he’s got leverage over me.

It’s all too much. That crack in my psyche widens, threatening to swallow me whole. The whispers of doubt, the warring feelings of rage and helplessness push me closer to the edge. I won't let this jerk think he can get one over on me. Especially not now. I take a deep breath, grounding myself in the moment, but it does little to quench the force building up.

Without thinking, I shove him.

The impact sends him sprawling against the rows of soda bottles, the clatter echoing through the store, a momentary silence swallowing the angry exchanges around us.

"You don't know who you're messing with!" I bark, my voice filling the space brightly, fueling the adrenaline racing through my veins.

He manages to push himself back to his feet, the cocky grin replaced with a flash of genuine surprise. "You want to throw punches? Then let's see what you've really got."

Before I can pause to reflect on what I'm doing, my fists fly at him again, this time landing a punch square against his jaw. The blow resonates in my knuckles, and I feel the immediate satisfaction of impact.

He stumbles back, shock rooting him to the floor for just a second. As reality snaps back into place, I immediately realize what I've done.

"What the hell?" he growls, wiping a trickle of blood from the corner of his mouth.

The playful demeanor is gone, replaced by a feral intensity that matches my own, and that ignites something primal inside me.

"Step back!" I shout, and yet there's a part of me that revels in the wildness of it all.

A feeling of power and control surges as the anger clouds my judgment. The stares of bystanders only throw gasoline on the fire.

"Think you're tough, huh?" he taunts, a hint of a challenge laced in his voice as he shifts his weight forward, readying himself.

But there's no backing down now. I will not let this guy make a fool of me.

Not here. Not today.

"You wanted to see the real Captain?" I ask. "You fucked around, and now you're about to find out."

Before I can process the situation, the two of us are tumbling into a chaotic melee. My fists swing wildly, and adrenaline floods my veins, drowning any remaining sense of caution or reason. I can barely distinguish between friend or foe as we crash into a nearby display, a cacophony of bottle explosions ringing in my ears.

"Back off!" I yell again, though this time it's not in reference to him, but the crowd that's started to encircle us, their whispers growing louder.

Adrenaline fuels my every movement, and I'm caught in a haze of aggression. It feels good to be the catalyst of chaos—to reclaim some control that has been stripped away from me since the accident.

With one swift motion, I shove him again. He crashes into rows of snacks, scattering chips and wrappers across the floor, and the satisfying crunch sends a rush through me.

I can't stop. I don't want to stop.

This feels right, even while a distant part of me screams in panic.

"Enough!" someone calls out, but the warning slides right past me.

I lunge forward again, throwing another punch, but something shifts in the crowd. Suddenly, hands grab my arms, pulling me back as someone shouts: "Security!"

And then it hits me. This isn't just some fight in a gas station. No, this is my life unraveling before my very eyes.

"Hey—let me go!" I yell, struggling against the grip holding me back. Rage surges within me as I fight against the hands restraining me.

"You're done, Captain! Step back! Now!" A voice booms from behind the crowd—an authoritative call that slices through the din, but I'm too far gone to listen.

My heart pounds in my chest, each beat syncing with the adrenaline coursing through my veins. I wriggle, desperate to free myself from the grip of those who've stepped in but only stoke the flames of my fury.

"I'll handle this. Get off me."

The man I confronted attempts to get back on his feet, eyes narrowed, now visibly furious. "You think you can just waltz in here and act like some tough guy? You don't know who you're messing with."

In the fray, there's a moment when I see his expression shift from anger to one of faint disbelief, and just that flicker pulls me back briefly. Real regret flashes through. This isn't who I am. Losing control like this. Not in front of witnesses. Not like this.

But then the swelling crowd, the voices echoing around me, stirs the chaos back alive, and I catch snippets of their thoughts about me.

"Isn't that Captain Teague?"

"He really snapped, didn't he?"

I can't wrap my head around it.

This isn't how it was supposed to be. With gritted teeth, I look toward the gas station cashier, who stands frozen in shock, a thin sheen of sweat beading on his forehead. This is not how I wanted to be seen. Not as a man engulfed in a violent altercation.

"Get him out of here!" one of the officers shouts, and suddenly I'm being dragged backward, away from the crowd.

I struggle against them, desperation clawing at my throat. "No! Let me go!"

"Enough already!" A second voice cuts through, this one coming from a uniformed officer, stepping in with authority as my vision narrows on the scene around me. "You've made your point. Now it's time to chill the hell out before you make this worse."

Worse—how could it possibly get worse? My mind swims in disarray.

As they lead me outside, I can feel the intense scrutiny of the crowd—eyes judging me, whispering, making assumptions they know nothing about. I shake my head, struggling against the hands gripping my arms, the humiliation washing over me in waves.

"I'm not a threat. I wasn't trying to hurt anyone." I protest, but the words seem futile, echoing in the vast emptiness where my self-control once resided.

Outside, the sun is shining too brightly, a stark contrast to the storm brewing inside me. I momentarily regain some clarity as I glance at the officers holding me back. Their expressions are unreadable, a mix of authority and concern.

"Captain Teague, you need to calm down, or we will have no choice but to take you in," one of the officers warns, his voice low and steady, cementing the reality that I am now on the precipice of serious consequences.

"What? To jail?" I snap back, venting my frustration. "For defending myself against a punk who thinks he can talk down to me?"

"I don't care what brought you to this point," the officer replies. "This isn't the way to handle your issues. Think about your career. Think about your wife. You know this is only going to complicate everything further."

Sierra. The name slices through me, immediate and brutal. The realization hits hard. This isn't just about me. My reckless behavior has consequences that extend beyond this base, beyond this moment. I force my breathing to slow, fighting against the overwhelming instincts driving me toward aggression.

"Let go of me," I say, the words coming out with a hint of exhaustion as I sag forward. "I need to talk to someone—to Brigadier General Benedict. He's my commanding officer."

The officers exchange glances, their grips loosening slightly.

How did it escalate to this? At what point did I lose sight of the man I swore I would be? Was it that stupid gas station guy, or was it when I punched the nightstand? Maybe it was sometime before. Probably so. It's all becoming a blur.

I swallow hard, the bitterness of shame catching in my throat. "I'll handle this. I need to speak to Benedict." The relentless pressure of judgment weighs heavily on me, but there's something more—something that stirs within as the thought of Sierra's worried expression resurfaces.

"I'm sorry. Truly. Please accept my apology. Tell the gas station owners I'll pay for the damages."

Chapter Fifteen

SIERRA

A sense of panic thrums through me as I make my way back to Quantico. I've spent countless hours pondering the best approach to reach out to Carl again. The past week has served as a stark reminder that waiting for Oscar to find his way back to normalcy is a solution that will never arrive on its own.

Traffic on the highway is heavier than expected, mirroring the turmoil within me. I grip the steering wheel tightly. I can't shake the feeling that I hold the key—if only I could unlock the door to the man I once knew.

When I arrive at the base, the familiarity of the surroundings brings both comfort and anxiety. I tell the MPs at the gate that I'm there to see Brigadier General Carl Benedict. They make a phone call, then wave me through.

My palms sweat as I enter the administration building, navigating the corridors until I reach Carl's office. I'm not sure whether Oscar is here, which worries me. If he sees me on base, he'll probably lose it.

I knock before stepping inside, my breath catching as I

find Carl buried beneath stacks of paperwork. Luckily, my husband is nowhere in sight.

"Dr. Mallory," Carl greets, looking up from his desk. "I didn't expect to see you today. I was surprised when I got the call from the gate."

"Sir, I need to talk. It's about Oscar again," I say. "It's urgent."

He gestures for me to sit, and I take a seat across from him, my stomach twisting with apprehension.

"What's happening now?" he asks.

I take a deep breath, recalling everything I've witnessed and felt over the past week since I last sat in this office. "He's not okay," I explain. "His behavior has become more erratic. I'm genuinely scared for him—and for me."

A shadow passes across Carl's expression, and I can see him processing my words.

"How, exactly?"

"His temper has escalated. He's angry all the time and lashes out, not just at objects but sometimes at me," I dare to admit, feeling the weight of shame creeping in. "I mean, he hasn't actually hit me ... yet. Maybe I'm overreacting. I don't think so."

Carl's brows furrow slightly, his gaze intense. "If you're feeling unsafe—"

"I'm managing," I cut in quickly. "But he needs help. I think he's in serious pain inside, and he can't seem to find a way to talk about it, or face it. Please, I'm begging you to find a way to push for him to see someone. You have the power to help."

He leans back in his chair, contemplating my plea, but something tells me he needs further convincing.

"Look, Dr. Mallory—"

"You can call me Sierra."

I feel like Carl and I have grown closer in the past few days, as if our shared worries about Oscar have bonded us.

"Okay, Sierra," he continues, "I told Captain Teague just this morning to see someone. I've blocked his access to this base until I can be sure he isn't a danger to himself or anyone else here. I've been witness to some of the erratic behavior you mention."

"Was he here?"

"No, but I spoke to him on the phone when he was close by. He reacted poorly to my decision to block his access to base, and I told him to calm down. If he's out of control, we can't have him around. It'll only escalate things."

"Escalate?" Panic creeps into my voice. "What happened?"

"He got into a confrontation at a gas station. Made a scene, threw some things. It's not the first time I've seen his temper flare, but it's concerning," Carl admits, his gaze never wavering from mine. "The officers who showed up to intervene decided to let him off with a warning, but if he's acting that way in public—"

"I get it." I cut him off, dread pooling deeper. "What can we do?" I lean forward, desperate for action. "You have to help him. Not just for the sake of the Corps, but for me, too. I can't lose him."

He studies me for a long moment, the silence heavy with understanding. "Talk to me. Help me understand what's going on. If you worry that he's a danger to you, I need concrete details. Is he frequently violent, or is this a new thing?"

I grapple with my thoughts, sorting through my memories of Oscar. “It’s been escalating since the helo crash—but in moments of anger, he’s tried to control it.”

Carl nods, and I can see he’s trying to connect the dots. “But he’s taken it too far, hasn't he?”

This is harder than I thought. “Yes. Things have gotten much worse recently. I don’t know if it’s PTSD or something more. Something’s changed in him, General—”

"Call me Carl."

"Okay." I smile, the gesture a small comfort. I think of him as Carl, anyway.

“I’ll look into it,” he says, but I can still see the doubt creeping into his eyes, uncertainty lingering around the edges of his expression.

“For Oscar’s sake, and ours,” I say urgently. “Can you push for him to see a psychologist or a psychiatrist, even if it’s just formally? Make sure he does it, rather than just suggest it, you know? Help him confront whatever darkness is swirling inside? If he doesn’t face it head-on, I fear we might lose him for good.”

"Aren't you a psychologist, Sierra?"

I nod. "Yes, but I'm a child psychologist, and a brand-spanking new one at that. I'm not trained to properly treat adults. Oscar needs to see someone who is. Someone experienced."

Carl leans forward, brows knit, considering my words. “Starting today, I need you to keep me posted on everything that’s happening. If he becomes violent with you out or if you feel the need to involve the police, I want to know about it. Can you promise me that?"

"Yes," I reply. It's a relief to know that Carl is hearing me. "There's one more thing."

"What?"

I fidget in my seat, unsure whether to say this here. After a quick debate in my head, I decide to be completely transparent. What do I have to lose, at this point?

"Oscar thinks the Marine Corps did this to him. I don't know the details, and I know he's paranoid, but it sounds like he blames the Corps," I explain.

Carl leans back in his chair. “What do you mean?”

I swallow hard, my throat tightening. “I think he believes there are shadows following him—like someone manipulated him or caused these changes in his behavior. He’s convinced there’s some larger conspiracy at play.”

“That’s a serious allegation,” Carl replies, his voice steady but cautious. “If he believes that, then we have to tread carefully. It raises red flags, and the situation could worsen quickly.”

“I understand,” I say quickly. “But I know my husband. He was tenacious even before all of this. If I don’t get him the help he needs, if I don’t intervene, I’m terrified of what might happen next. I feel like everything is spiraling.”

Carl’s expression shifts slightly. “How has he handled stress in the past? Did he show signs of this kind of behavior before the crash?”

“Never like this,” I admit, shaking my head. “Not even close. Oscar has always been fiery, but it was manageable. He could usually talk about what roiled inside him. But now? Now, it feels like it’s festering under the surface, escalating with each passing day. Each passing hour, really.”

“Then we need to make sure he’s seen. I’ll do everything I

can to help him get the care he needs. Just understand that he needs to be willing to participate, too."

"What if he refuses?"

"I'll make the arrangements, and I'll ensure Dr. Caleb Grenier, our head psychiatrist, reaches out to him directly. A prescription might be in order. If nothing else, Dr. Grenier's attention might help dispel the notion that your husband is being targeted."

Relief washes over me, a flicker of hope igniting in my chest. "Thank you," I say earnestly. "That means a lot. I truly can't lose him."

He meets my gaze, his expression softening. "Just be careful, okay? I'm concerned about *you*. If you feel like you're in physical danger, go to a domestic violence shelter. Would you like the name—?"

"That won't be necessary."

I say my goodbyes to Carl, and he gives me a polite squeeze of the shoulder. I get the idea he wants to hug me, but doesn't want to be unprofessional. I appreciate his kindness more than he knows. Finally, I feel like maybe I'm not alone in this. Between Carl and Beth, perhaps I've found the support I need to make it through.

On the drive home, I decide to call my parents again. I miss them. If things weren't so crazy, I'd be inviting them up for a visit. We don't usually go this long without one or the other of us traveling to spend time.

I take a deep breath and dial their number. It rings for a few moments before Mom answers, her voice bright with surprise. "Sierra! Oh, it's so good to hear from you! How are you?"

"I'm okay, Mom," I reply, trying to keep my voice steady.

"I've been meaning to call back since I didn't have a chance to talk to Dad last time. I miss you guys."

"We miss you too! Hold on. Let me get him on the phone." I hear a scratching noise as she covers the receiver, then, "Marty! Your daughter is on the line. Come talk!"

I can practically hear Dad's warm smile when he joins the call. They still use a landline, which means they're on receivers in different rooms.

"Hey, kiddo!" Dad says. "How's life in our nation's capital?"

I chuckle. He always says it like a TV game show host. Like he's giving away an all-expenses-paid vacation or something.

"Pretty good. It's warming up a little bit. The sun has been out."

We proceed to chat for a few minutes about the upcoming arrival of spring, Dad's desire to get in the pool when it's warm enough, and the new book club Mom has joined.

"How's Oscar?" she asks when there's a lull in the conversation, her tone shifting to concern.

The question hangs in the air, heavy with unspoken implications. I hesitate, struggling to find the balance between honesty and protecting my husband. "He's been having a challenging time lately," I say at last. "But I think he's getting the help he needs. I just wanted to reach out and touch base with you. Don't worry about me. Everything is going to be okay."

I think they might ask questions, but they move on.

"Have you considered coming home for a visit?" Mom asks. "It might help to clear your mind."

"We'd love to see you," Dad adds. "Remember what I've always said—no matter how big you get, you'll always be our baby."

"I know," I say, biting back tears.

"We could come to you, if that's easier," Mom says. "The Cherry Blossom Festival is coming up next month, right?"

"That's right," I say. "I'd love to have you here for that. It's my favorite time of the year in D.C., and I was too busy unpacking to really enjoy it last spring. Let me talk to Oscar about his schedule. I'll let you know."

We talk a while longer, reminiscing about my childhood. I tell them how much I love them and appreciate what a wonderful support they've always been for me, and they tell me how happy they are to have had a daughter. Usually, Mom asks if Oscar and I are thinking of having children of our own. She doesn't mention it this time, although I get the sense that it's on the tip of her tongue.

As we say our goodbyes and I end the call, I'm overwhelmed with gratitude for the good people in my life. I might be going through a challenging time, but my life is beautiful.

This, too, shall pass, one way or another.

Chapter Sixteen

OSCAR

I pull into the driveway, my hands still trembling from the confrontation I had at the gas station. The sun is out, and I almost resent the day for going on so long, even though I know that doesn't make logical sense. A gnawing tightness coils in my gut as I step out of the car and make my way to the front door.

I know Sierra will be waiting for me. I've been gone for hours, driving around to try and sort things in my mind. She probably wonders where I've been. I wince at the thought. It feels like another curious wrinkle hangs in the air between us.

As I step inside, the familiar scent of her hair and perfume hits me, but the comfort feels like a cruel reminder of all that I've buried underneath layers of anger and confusion. Gripping the doorknob tight, I take a deep breath to steady myself.

"Sierra?" I call out, trying to sound casual, forcing my voice to be steady. "Honey, I'm home."

As I scan the house, I realize it's unnaturally quiet. No sounds of movement, no laughter or warmth spilling from the kitchen. My stomach knots as I glance over at the kitchen where dinner preparations would usually be underway. Our home, once filled with joyous clatter, feels like a husk of what once was. It's a stark reminder of the chasm that has formed.

The knot tightens further as I head towards the living room. That's where I find it—her stuff scattered around the coffee table, papers and a few books she had read piled haphazardly. I run my hand through my short hair, frustration mounting like a storm cloud.

"Damn it, what the fuck is this?" I mutter, shoving a stack of papers to the side. The sudden need to destroy something—anything—rises within me as panic gnaws at my thoughts.

Was she seriously not here? Did she go out? Did she leave? I didn't enter through the garage, so I didn't notice whether her car was there.

The questions spiral, overwhelming me with uncertainty. I focus on the coffee table, subconsciously letting the anger boil up. I grip the edge of it, my knuckles turning white. "Why aren't you here, Sierra?" I hiss aloud, needing her presence, needing her voice to calm the whirlwind clawing inside me.

And then it happens. My frustration bursts, escaping through my fingertips, my body reacting before my mind can catch up. I slam the palm of my hand down against the table, and it tips dangerously to the side.

The table wobbles precariously before crashing back down, sending the books tumbling, pages flapping like frightened birds. The sound reverberates through the empty house, lingering in the air.

"Just ... stop it!" I yell at myself, the words bitter in my throat, echoing the stupidity of letting my anger guide me.

The knot in my gut tightens further as I pace the room, my pulse pounding. Where the hell is she? A sudden imagining pulls at the edges of my mind—what if she's out there, discussing me with someone else? What if she's realizing how unworthy I am of her?

These thoughts claw at my sanity.

I stride through the house, the silence magnifying my growing sense of dread. I shove aside the setting of the dinner she wasn't there to prepare, knocking over a bowl in the process. It tumbles loudly.

As I turn to the hallway, my eyes catch on the mantle where a framed photo of the two of us sits, our faces radiant with love and bliss. It brings back a wave of emotion that crashes over me, sharp and jarring. I take a step forward, reaching towards it.

But the moment shifts. My emotions darken as uncertainty pricks at me, reminding me of everything I've lost and everything that's slipping through my fingers.

"Stop!" I roar, flinging the frame across the room. The glass shatters, splinters exploding across the wooden floor, shards tumbling like broken dreams.

Then I hear it—a noise coming from the back of the house. I freeze, my muscles tense. Footsteps? Did she come back? A part of me wants to run, but I'm anchored to the floor, rooted by my anger.

"Where have you been?" I shout, anger spilling into my voice again as I confront the sound. The shadows in the hallway seem to shift, dancing with my fury.

I stalk back through the house, reaching the living room just as she steps in from the kitchen, confusion spilling across her face. I see her, standing there, wide-eyed and uncertain, and the realization hits me like a freight train. She's back, but there's a heightened fear in her gaze that I haven't seen before.

"I thought I told you to stay away!" The words rip from my mouth unconsciously. I don't even know why I said them, but the primal instinct to assert dominance blooms within me.

"What are you talking about? I was just—" Sierra starts, the anxiety in her voice rising like the tension between us.

I interrupt her, unable to keep the words at bay. "You were *just* what? Out? Out running errands? Out trying to distraction yourself from what's happening right here?" The words tumble out, harsh and unyielding.

She tries to step forward, to assert her presence, but I can see the hesitation, the way her confidence wavers. "Oscar, I was going to make us dinner ..." She gestures vaguely toward the kitchen. "I wanted to surprise you with your favorite."

My anger surges again, fueled by the insecurity clawing at my sides. "And what? You thought you'd feel better by pretending everything is fine?" I take a step toward her, voice low and threatening. "You think this is going to work if you avoid the reality we're in?"

I see her flinch, and it's like a cold slap to my face, a sudden shift in clarity that breaks through the haze of anger that surrounds me.

"Stop," she says, voice shaking slightly. "You're scaring me!"

And those words—her admission—crash against the wall I've built. It sends a jolt rushing through my mind, but the anger is too potent, thrumming like a live wire. Instead of stepping back, I step closer, the instinct pulling me dangerously toward the precipice.

"Am I scaring you?" I growl, closing the distance. "You think that's what I want? Do you think that's how I want you to look at me?"

"I just wanted to make things right!" she cries out, hands clenched at her sides. "Why can't you see me? Why can't you just snap out of this darkness you're in?"

Her words strike something deep inside of me, a flickering ember of awareness, but I can hardly process it before I feel the anger swell once again, blind and wild. This is my home. I built these walls, fought tooth and nail for my place here, and yet somehow, she treats my descent into madness as something flimsy to dismiss. Something she can just brush aside.

In my mind, that familiar voice comes back.

Who have I turned into? Where have I lost myself?

With every confrontational step forward, all I see is the fear slowly etching her features—a bitter reminder of the distance I've created. Anger surges, electrifying and reckless, but I can't shake the feeling that I'm being swallowed whole by something beyond my control.

"You don't understand!" I shout, shoving my hands through my hair in exasperation. "You're not in my head. You don't know what it's like."

Sierra's expression darkens, and in that moment, she doesn't just look scared. She looks hurt.

"I'm trying to help you, Oscar. But you're pushing me away." Her voice trembles as she raises it, desperate to be heard. "You say you can handle this, but it's clear that you can't. You don't have to fight me. You should be fighting whatever's going on inside of you."

At her words, I feel the walls around me begin to collapse, the defensive armor I wore for so long cracking and peeling away. I don't know how to voice this turmoil, this deep sense of disarray. The contrast between the man I aspire to be and the one I'm becoming feels too heavy to bear.

"I'm not the one who's fighting!" I shout back, frustration threatening to choke me like a vice from all sides. "You think I wanted any of this? I didn't choose to change. None of this was my choice."

As her fear transforms into something else—exasperation, maybe?—the line dividing us grows even thicker. "So what? You're just going to go on living in some psychotic haze, destroying everything we have?"

Tension thickens, and I can feel the world spinning around me, slowly unraveling like a thread being pulled from a garment. Something snaps in me, a visceral reaction that's beyond my control.

"I'm done pretending. If I can't even be me, then why should you care?"

Without thinking, I swing my arm, rage erupting like a volcano as I knock over a lamp on the nearby table. The object shatters against the floor, each piece a violent reminder of what could easily happen next.

Sierra's eyes widen as if the very essence of who I am to her, the love we built together, is fracturing.

"What the hell?" she cries, shrinking back as shards of porcelain scatter around us. I can feel her fear. "You can't keep doing this. Can't you see how far you've gone?"

I can feel the anger bubbling inside me, furious energy demanding release. "It doesn't matter," I mutter, barely registering her words as I step forward again. I'm angry with myself. Angry with her. Angry with the world for not understanding how lost I am.

"Stop!" she exclaims again, her voice stronger this time, yet still laced with fear. "You don't have to act like this! You're better than this!"

"Better? Is that what you think?" I challenge, my voice low and menacing. "You act like I chose this path. I didn't have a choice. I was forced into this. I'm trapped!"

The words tumble out of my mouth before I can stop them, and I see Sierra's expression shift again, her unwavering resolve now peppered with empathy. But I'm not ready for that yet. The pressure building inside me only urges me further, compelling me to lash out, to push harder.

I scoff. "Look at how you walk around here like everything is fine, acting as if you can hold my hand through it all. But do you really understand what I'm going through? Do you even care?"

Shock flashes across her face. "Of course, I care. You're my husband. Every time you lash out, every time you hurt things, you're distancing yourself from me. I want to help you. I'm trying desperately to help you."

"Stop saying that word!" I yell, covering my ears with both hands.

"Help?"

All I can hear is the pounding of furious blood in my temples, drowning out her pleas.

"You think I can just take your hand and walk back into this life like nothing's changed?" I ask. "That we can stay on the merry-go-round while I'm unraveling? No! I'm sick of pretending!"

Something in my voice shifts, and a feeling dark as night wraps around my core. I take another step forward, and Sierra's back hits the end of the couch, her eyes wide with shock.

"I want you back, Oscar!" she shouts, her tone fierce, though the quiver in her voice betrays the fear that underscores her proclamation. "You're pushing everyone away, though, and at this rate, it'll be too late."

Her words volley back and forth between us until they hit me like a punch to the gut. I can barely process them. The truth stabs at my heart, igniting an ache deep within where the fragments of who I once was reside.

"Aren't we already too late?" I hiss, anger bleeding into sorrow. "I can't even recognize myself anymore! I can't pretend I'm okay!"

I can sense her energy shifting again. She's scared—no, terrified—but more than that, she's resolute. It's infuriating and heartbreaking all at once.

"Do you think I haven't been scared myself?" she fires back, her voice sharp and unwavering. "Do you think I'm naive enough to simply sit back and let you destroy everything we've built together? I'm trying, Oscar Teague. I'm fighting for us, but you need to stop fighting against me."

Suddenly, I'm overcome with a rush of rage. That flicker of hope she carries only makes the struggle feel more insurmountable. I can't let this moment hang in the air any longer. Instinctively, I take another step forward, and in a sudden movement, I lash out again without thinking.

"Just stop!" I yell, my hand striking out, but it's only meant to push her away—an instinct born from fear and confusion rather than deliberate intent.

Before I can process what I'm doing, my hand grazes her face, not with intention to hurt, but the momentum sends her careening back toward the coffee table. The world seems to slow as I watch her knock into the edge, the impact catching me completely off-guard.

"Sierra!" I shout, panic rushing through me as she falls against the hard tabletop. Time halts for a beat, but then it crashes back into motion as her head strikes the corner, a sickening thud echoing through my senses.

Everything shatters.

Chapter Seventeen

SIERRA

There's a flicker of light, a jolt of pain, and … nothing.

My eyes are closed, it seems, and I'm falling, tumbling backward into a void as the world around me fades into a blur of colors and sounds.

The focus of reality is lost to me, and I grasp for something, anything, to anchor me. My mind races, and I feel it all —the gaping terror, the confusion, the realization that something has gone terribly wrong.

Time stretches and contracts around me in chaotic pulses, distorting the fabric of existence. I am suspended between worlds—one that is vibrant and alive, filled with the love and laughter that once defined my marriage, and another that is cold and unforgiving, a shadowed abyss that I don't understand.

No! I scream inwardly, a soundless cry swallowed by the growing dark. The weight of it presses down on me, suffocating in its silence.

"Sierra!"

A voice pierces through the haze, slapping against the walls of my consciousness.

It's his voice. Oscar's voice, calling my name, but I can't reach him.

The world shifts dizzyingly, and I catch fleeting glimpses of our home. Everything echoes back in stark clarity, weaving between the fading shadows of fear. I see our wedding day—Oscar's smile, the soft light catching the gold in my ring as it glimmered with promise.

Another image flashes, sharp and jarring: the moment I told him I was afraid. His face contorted into something alien, rage and pain twisting together as the edges of our once-beautiful life began to fray.

"Sierra, stay with me!"

The voice again. It's more frantic now, a plea filled with panic and anguish.

But darkness seeps in, and the tumult of color fades, leaving only an encroaching blackness. My breath quickens as I feel myself slipping away, the warmth of life draining from my veins.

"Please ... don't let go!"

His voice sounds raw, and I want to respond, to assure him that I'm here, that I won't leave. But there is an immovable heaviness in my limbs. I'm not in control here.

I start to float. The memories swirl around me, each one its own flickering light amidst the encroaching void. I grasp at them desperately, wanting to hold on, to remember everything—the laughter, the love, the beautiful moments.

Then suddenly, I'm back, it seems. I feel a pulling sensation, sort of like the splash landing after being tossed down a waterslide.

When I open my eyes, everything is just as I'd left it.

The sun is shining, the birds are singing, and the scent of fresh coffee lingers in the air. Life, as it seems, goes on.

But something isn't right. The shadows are too sharp, the colors too bright. The air feels heavy, like I'm breathing through a thick, invisible fog. Not to mention, I'm hovering several feet higher than the ground Oscar stands on. It's as if the place where I now exist is on a higher plane.

That's when I realize.

Oh, God.

I'm dead.

The notion settles over me like a heavy cloak, suffocating yet almost comforting in its finality.

I drift between memories and shadows, an echo of who I once was. I'm suspended in a liminal space, making an ever-diminishing distinction between life and oblivion.

It feels like I'm crying, even though tears can no longer fall from my eyes.

In this ethereal place, I hear Oscar's voice breaking the silence, full of despair and longing. Each cry reverberates through the open void. I want to reach for him, to pull him out of this darkness, but waves of sorrow wash over me with every attempt.

Images of our love flicker brightly—the day we met, the laughter echoing through the summer air, the tender kisses beneath the glowing moonlight. Yet with every recollection comes a growing sense of loss. Slowly, I realize that the beautiful life we crafted together is slipping through the cracks of a shattered reality.

"Don't go!"

I want to scream in return, to tell Oscar that I can't

simply vanish, that I want to stay, but the words drown in the heavy silence surrounding me. Instead, I float through the fog, searching for clarity, for something to hold on to that connects me back to him and the memories.

The shadows grow heavier. No longer do the moments pulse with the warmth of life. Now they swirl coldly, whispering doubts and fears that gnaw my essence. I see flashes of fear in Oscar's eyes, flashes that remind me of every time I felt pulled further from the core of who we once were. He's a man lost in confusion, battling demons under the guise of sanity.

I linger there, hovering in that smothering darkness, but then a flicker catches my eye. A soft light amidst the black.

I reach for it, feeling the warmth against my hand.

"Stay with me," I try to whisper back. "I'm here, just in some strange new disguise ... like Ralph Waldo Emerson said."

"Please!"

I wrestle with the memories as they intertwine. Can he feel the despair that clings to me? I push against the heaviness, my voice stronger this time.

"I'm here! I'm here!"

But just like that, the light begins to fade. The warmth disappears.

Time bends in this new reality, stretching out like a formless shadow. I feel as though I'm caught in a web woven from both despair and longing, hanging in the balance between two worlds—one filled with vibrant memories and the other shrouded in darkness.

I can no longer feel my body, no longer sense the familiar weight of my skin or the comforting pulse of breath filling my lungs. All I have left are the emotions, raw and unyielding. And yet, they ripple like water, shifting beneath the surface as I hover in this in-between state.

"Oscar," I call out, my voice lost in the ether, a desperate echo that reaches nowhere.

My heart, or what's left of it, aches with the want to reach him, to break through the veil of this ethereal fog and tell him that he isn't alone. Each yearning call only pulls me further into the shadows, amplifying the isolation I feel.

The world shifts around me, and the memories continue to swirl with blinding speed.

In one instant, I'm at our wedding, the joyous laughter ringing in my ears, and in the next, I'm alongside him in the kitchen, the scent of a sumptuous meal wafting around us like a comforting embrace.

Yet even the warmth of those memories begins to fade. What remains is a sense of unsettling dread.

The evening unfolds before me as I slip quietly through the walls of our home, observing as he stumbles through making a dinner that isn't just a meal anymore. It's a moment of desperation.

He must not realize that I'm gone from my body.

I watch him cook as if in a trance, every movement mechanical and distant. Oscar's face wears a mask of concentration that does little to disguise the turmoil brewing just below the surface. The love that once radiated from him now feels dulled, flickering like a candle's flame struggling against the wind.

I see him chopping vegetables with a fierce intensity. Each slice is punctuated by hurried breaths. There's something unsettling about it, a silent chaos that swirls around him.

I fear what will happen to him now that he's left alone. It feels like he isn't safe with himself. Like someone should protect him. Like *I* should protect him.

"Oscar?" I whisper.

He doesn't hear me, or perhaps he can't. He stirs the pot on the stove, glancing over his shoulder as if sensing a presence that somehow lingers just outside his grasp. The shadows dance around him, wrapping tight with unyielding uncertainty. I wish desperately for him to break free.

"Please, talk to me," I murmur, hovering nearby. "I'm still here, my love."

My heart aches at the sight of him, so close yet so painfully distant. I want to scream, to shake him awake from this fog that's enveloping him, from the dark thoughts that taunt his very existence. But my voice ricochets against the invisible barrier that separates us.

As he stirs, I catch glimpses of his thoughts—a turbulent sea of pain and confusion battling within him. I sense his growing fear that he's lost me for good. The uncertainty gnaws at him, yet he lacks the clarity to confront it.

He pours what looks like a delicious sauce into the pan, his brow furrowed in concentration. It's a beautiful dish, but soured by the circumstances. Each movement is frantic, desperate, as though he's trying to conjure warmth into the bones of our home.

I take a step closer, wanting to envelop him in love and assurance, to remind him that beneath the turmoil, there is a bond stronger than fear—stronger than the darkness wrapping its talons around him.

"Don't you see it?" I ask, my voice choking with the

intensity of my longing. "You don't have to fight against the shadows alone. I'm here. I'm always here."

But he stirs, his expression twisting in frustration, as if he can feel my presence yet cannot reach it. Sort of like a half-formed thought.

"Why can't she just wake up?" he mutters under his breath, and I feel my soul rip apart.

He's speaking to the air, speaking to nothing, and the sorrow in his voice sends shards of grief splintering through my own being. He is lost in his own mind.

Truly and utterly lost.

Without warning, he slams down the spoon, the clatter echoing through the kitchen. He runs a trembling hand through his hair, his face shadowed in despair.

"This isn't how it's supposed to be," he whispers, a rough edge to his voice.

I wish I could take this torment from him.

I drift closer, wanting so fiercely to reach him, to break through the veil of confusion that blankets our space. "Oscar ..." I whisper, though I know he can't hear me in the way I wish he could. "I'm here."

But he turns away, shaking his head as though shaking off my words. "If I could just get it right," he murmurs, his voice cracking with frustration. "What am I supposed to do?"

My heart aches at the sight of him, this man I love battling the shadows of his own mind. I desperately want to comfort him, to pull him out of this spiraling madness—but how? I reach out, hoping my spirit could somehow bridge the chasm between us.

But my hand passes through his shoulder like smoke. He doesn't flinch. Doesn't even blink.

The disappointment is a crushing blow. *Ouch.*

"You can talk to me," I implore once again, pouring all my love into that whisper. "You don't have to hide your thoughts beneath layers of anger."

The kitchen grows still, save for the faint bubbling of the sauce on the stove. For an instant—I swear—I see the flicker of recognition in his eyes, as if he were on the cusp of understanding that I am still a part of him, still woven into the fabric of his being.

Just as quickly, it vanishes, swallowed by the depths of his despair.

He picks up a wine glass, pouring a generous amount before tossing it back in one hurried motion. The liquid shimmers as it disappears down his throat.

"Please, Oscar," I murmur. "Drowning your troubles in alcohol won't help."

I don't know what I want from him, exactly.

Actually, I do know.

Relief. I want relief.

He slams the glass down on the counter, the shattering sound deafening in that moment, and I cringe at the violence, though it's not directed at me. "I can't take this anymore!" he shouts, voice laced with all-consuming anger. "She was here! She should be here! Why isn't she waking up?"

"Oscar, I never left you," I plead softly.

But it's no use. I am gone from his world.

Chapter Eighteen

OSCAR

I pace back and forth in the kitchen, the sharp scent of food filling the air. I'm trying to keep things together, to function as if this is just a typical evening—just another ordinary night cooking for my wife. There's a sense of desperate normalcy that I'm clinging to, a fragile layer of reality I refuse to let shatter any further.

My thoughts keep spiraling.

I can fix this. I can still bring her back. She's just sleeping.

I glance over at the living room where she lies, a gentle figure bathed in the soft glow of the lamp. Her stillness would almost be serene if it weren't for the nagging sensation deep within me. The conversation earlier echoes in my mind, but I push it away.

This is just a temporary setback.

I hasten to pour another glass of wine, hoping it might clear my thoughts, but the bottle feels heavy in my hands. I will not let my mind turn against me.

Just as I take a sip, the doorbell rings, slicing through the stillness like a knife.

Who the fuck could that be? I set down the glass with a sudden clatter and stride through the hallway, a wave of irritation washing over me.

"Who is it?" I shout, opening the door before anyone can answer.

Beth stands there, her face lit with a hint of concern that twitches at the edges of her traits. "Oscar! I was in the area, and I thought I'd check on you two. Can I come in?"

Her brightness is a momentary light, but panic rises at her presence. What if she sees?

"Sierra's sleeping," I say, forcing a casual tone. I can feel the unease ripple through me.

"Sleeping?" she asks, tilting her head as a hint of worry spreads across her features. "What time did she turn in? Is everything okay?"

"She's fine," I insist, my voice edging on defensive. "You don't need to worry about her. She's been working too hard recently. Just needs her rest, that's all."

Beth looks unconvinced, her brow knitting together. She knows that Sierra doesn't have a job. I should have come up with a better excuse.

"Can I come in? I'd love to see both of you," she says sweetly, yet her eyes are scrutinizing.

I try to block her path, panic surging. "Really, Beth, it's not a good time. You don't realize how tired I am. I just ... need some space right now." But even as I say it, I know it's a weak response. My heart races, and I wish I could convince her to leave before she discovers the truth.

"Space?" she echoes, her voice laced with disbelief. "Oscar, are you sure everything is all right? You sound ... off. Let me in."

Before I can stop her, she pushes past me, stepping into the dimly lit foyer. I can almost feel the heat of her gaze on me, probing, searching for answers I can't provide.

"Beth, really, it's not necessary—" I insist, but she's already making her way toward the living room.

"Hey! If you don't want to talk, that's fine, but I'm not leaving until I can make sure Sierra's okay," she calls back over her shoulder, a hint of determination in her tone.

I want to stop her, but panic seizes me as she rounds the corner, leaving me rooted to the spot. "Sierra!" I call out, a knot twisting in my stomach. "Sierra, can you hear me?"

And then I hear Beth gasp from the living room, the sharp intake of breath slicing through the tension that hangs in the air.

"What the hell, Oscar?" she shouts. I rush to follow her into the living room, dread creeping into my limbs.

I find her standing there, eyes wide, mouth agape as she stares at the scene in disbelief. "What happened?"

"She's fine!" I shout, panic lacing my voice as I step between her and Sierra's still figure. "She's just resting. There's nothing wrong."

"Nothing wrong?" Beth's expression shifts from shock to a fierce determination. "You're delusional, Oscar. She's not just sleeping. You need to call for help."

"Help?" I bark incredulously. There's that fucking word again. "Why would I call for help? She's been tired. That's all. Get out of my way." I try to push past her, but she stands her ground.

Beth argues, raising her voice. "For God's sake, Oscar! Do you even realize what's happening right now? Make sense! This isn't normal!"

"I told you, she's just—" My voice falters as the harsh reality of her words sinks in, my denial crumbling around me.

She pushes past me again, going out the front door this time. "I'm calling 9-1-1."

My heart races, dread flooding my entire being as I watch her grab her phone and begin to dial. "You can't do that." I say, panic rolling through me like a tidal wave. "Beth, please. You don't understand."

She doesn't look up, her focus unwavering on the call. Her body is tense, her stance fierce. "I don't care what you think I understand. Something is very wrong here, and you need help. She—"

"Stop!" I yell, anger twisting tightly around me. "You don't have to involve anyone. Just ... just let me deal with this. I'm figuring it out."

"Deal with what, Oscar? Are you not seeing what's in front of you?" The intensity of her gaze feels like fire and ice at once. "Sierra is dead, and you're not going to convince me otherwise. I'm not leaving her like this."

"Let me handle my own wife," I grind out, trying to maintain some semblance of authority, lest the truth of the nightmare come to light. "You don't understand what you're doing."

As she steps back, her voice raises even higher, filled with an assertiveness that surprises me. "Oscar! You're not in a position to make decisions for her—look around you. She's dead! Dead!"

"What do you want me to say?" I snap, my voice rising in disbelief, frustration bubbling dangerously as I whirl around to face her. "She's taking a nap. I mean, it's been a long day."

Beth's face twists in horror, incredulity fueling her

resolve. "A nap? Are you out of your mind right now?" She presses the call button, eyes flaring with determination.

"Don't you dare!" My voice breaks, a desperate plea laced with anguish. "I'll lose her. I *can't* lose her."

"You're being irrational!" she cries, panic edging into her tone while she speaks. "Go and sit down somewhere. Police will be here soon."

In that moment, I want to shake sense into her, to make her understand that calling anyone means losing more than I'm willing to allow. I blink rapidly, the gravity of my emotions making it increasingly difficult to breathe.

I step closer, the desperation clawing at my throat. "Beth, you don't understand. She might wake up. I've spent every moment since she hit her head waiting for her to come back to me, and now you're ruining everything."

Her eyes widen, the shock twisting her features into a mask of concern and anger.

"I know her! I know Sierra!" I shout, my voice a mix of fury and plea. "She just needs time. She needs me."

There's a tense silence as she processes my words. "Oscar, please. The reality is right in front of you. Denial isn't going to bring her back. You need to face this. Let someone who can help take over."

"No one understands!" I roar, the raw words spilling out before I can catch them. "You think I'm okay with this? You think I'm just pretending? I felt her! I was with her!"

"I don't care what you felt. She needs—"

"Then why can't I feel anything now?" I interrupt, panic spilling over. "I'm losing ground by the second! I can't let her go!"

"Let go of what?" she counters fiercely. "Of the idea that

she's still waking up? Oscar!" Her voice wavers, but she pulls it back. "Please, just ... let the professionals take it from here. They're on their way."

"Get off my property!" I shout suddenly, voice brimming with both terror and anger. "Get out of here before I do something you'll regret."

With those words, everything shifts. The despair and the anger echoes, ricocheting back at me. I want to scream, to grasp for control, but I don't know how to break the chains that bind me to this awful fate.

Beth doesn't back down. "I am not leaving her here like this, Oscar. You need to understand that, no matter what you think you can do on your own. She was my best friend."

Tears fill her eyes, and the intensity of her emotion startles me.

I take a halting breath, every ounce of my being forcing me to find some shred of calm. "She's not dead, Beth. She's sleeping."

Within seconds, I hear the sirens and a police cruiser comes to a stop in front of the house. A young African American woman in uniform gets out, gun raised and pointed in my direction.

Panic floods my voice as the officer approaches. "You have to understand! She's not—"

"Keep your hands where I can see them," the officer commands, voice steady and authoritative as she approaches, a hint of concern in her eyes.

"No, you don't get it!" I flare, emotions boiling over. "She's just resting! You can't take her away from me!" I can feel desperation clawing at my throat.

"What's going on here?" another young officer asks as he

gets out of the cruiser, taking in the scene at a glance—me, wild-eyed and frantic, Beth pale and steadfast. His gun is raised and now pointed at me, too.

I lead the officers into the house, heart racing, trapped between the echoes of my own unraveling and the sharp tang of impending reality crashing down around me. "She's fine! Just ... just let me explain!"

"Ma'am," the first officer says, directing her attention back to Beth, who has followed us inside and stands firm in my line of sight. "Are you hurt? What's happening here?"

"She's not all right. Obviously. He's in denial. She's dead. Something happened before I got here. I'm a friend. I stopped by to check on her." Beth's voice quakes as she points towards Sierra's motionless figure.

My panic climbs to an unbearable level as I feel the emotions from the two police officers reel back towards me.

"No! You can't say that!" I plead. "I promised her I'd be here when she woke up! She's just sleeping!"

The officers exchange glances, and I can see questions simmering hidden beneath the surface, weighing every assessment they make of the situation. They must think I'm insane —that I don't know how to process the reality of my wife lying unresponsive.

Maybe I am and maybe I don't

"Sir, we need to assess the situation," the first officer says, taking her cue to step forward. My heart thrums wildly in my chest.

Whatever happens next, I have to control the narrative. I have to bring Sierra back.

"Get away from her! She's not dead!"

"Oscar, please," Beth implores, her eyes pleading even

though her tone is sharp. "You need to let them help. You're not okay."

I turn to her, anguish twisting within me. "I can't lose her, Beth."

A weighty silence fills the air, punctuated only by the distant sound of sirens ringing. More cops.

The tension coils tighter, every moment stretching painfully thin.

The officers exchange another glance that says more than words could carry. It's the kind of look that reads: *We have to do something.*

"Sir," the first officer speaks again, her voice more measured now, "we need to check on her, to determine her condition. I understand this may be hard for you, but we have to do our jobs."

"No!" I plead as I throw myself to the floor and cling to my wife's dead body like a madman. "You don't have to do this! You're not seeing what I see. She's just resting. She's going to wake up any minute now."

I'm repeating myself, which makes me sound even crazier. I hear it. I know that.

"Sir, please," the woman says. "Step back."

Her words feel like a chasm opening before me, a reminder of the descent into chaos awaiting me if I let them take her away. I can already feel the darkness creeping back, swallowing every piece of logic I might hold onto.

"Stop, please!" I shout, my voice raw with desperation. "You don't know her! You don't know how she is! I do! I promise she's fine!"

But in that moment, I can see the officers' resolve hardening, and I realize that the battle I'm waging is against reality itself. A reality that feels unbearable to acknowledge.

"Sir, step back right now," the other officer commands, his voice steady, a grounding force in the chaos. "We need to assess the situation, and you're making it difficult for us to do so."

With a swell of emotions, something sharp surfaces. I can feel the boiling point nearing, a weight pressing relentlessly against my chest. Frustrations boil over like a simmering pot. I stand and take a step forward, defiance igniting my every muscle.

"You think you can just waltz in here and take her from me? You don't know what I've done for her." Each word drips with anger and desperation, and I can see the officers tighten slightly, hands hovering above their weapons.

"Everything isn't fine!" One officer shouts back. "You need to calm down, sir. Step back."

Before I can argue any more, both officers come at me. I feel a jolt of electricity and I spasm with pain for several excruciating seconds before I fall to the ground, unable to move.

Those assholes tased me. I guess I deserved that.

Chapter Nineteen

SIERRA

So, this is what it's like, I think to myself. *I've always wondered.*

I can't say the experience is a good one, so far. Maybe if I'd had more time to prepare, I wouldn't be in such shock. I'm struggling to adjust.

The world continues to dim around me, swirling shadows amplifying the suffocating silence that blankets the room. Shards of shattered memories ripple through the darkness, and I feel myself hovering at the edge—trapped between the echoes of what was and the heavy weight of what is.

A crack of thunder rumbles in my ears, pulling me into the spiral of chaos unfolding just beyond my reach as police work to secure the scene. I can sense Oscar's fervent scream reverberating through the void, a distant echo tinged with desperation.

"Stop! You don't understand!"

Every syllable pierces through me like daggers, sending pangs of anguish racing through my soul. I still want to respond, to tell him that I'm here and that I never left him, but I remain suspended in this abyss. I'm unable to break through the barrier that keeps me tethered to the shadows.

The air is thick with sorrow and uncertainty, and I witness the frantic rush of police shadows moving through the space, their voices clouded in disarray. "Sir, step back!" one shouts, while another pleads for calmness.

I drift closer, drawn by the weight of the moment, the chaos intensifying around us.

"Oscar!" I scream inside, pushing against the shrouded darkness, the very essence of my being tugging toward him.

He's been incapacitated by their tasers once, but he's recovering. I don't want them to hurt him.

He stands. His figure teeters uncertainly, emotions swirling like a tempest within him. He's a man breaking under the pressure, grasping for reality as it slips through his fingers. I see him resist the officers as they work to escort him out of the house, but within seconds, something shifts, and anger erupts once more.

"I told you, she's fine!" he yells, lashing out again. "You're making a mistake by being here!"

The officers move cautiously to restrain him, but I can feel his fury fizzing through the air like a grenade on the verge of detonation. I want nothing more than to break the silence and assure him that he isn't alone.

As they close in, the murmurs of concern swirl around the room like a lost incantation.

"Sir, are you armed?" one asks.

"Let me go!" Oscar shouts, voice rising.

"Call for more backup," one officer urges, though it's a phrase I barely catch through the growing chaos. "And medical assistance."

Backup? Medical assistance? Everything around me feels tangled and distorted. I want to scream, to wake my Oscar up from the nightmare we're both in, but my voice is lost in the ether between realms.

"You can't take her from me!" he cries, thrashing against their hold. "You don't understand! She's alive!"

The weight of his words resonates in the air, battling against the suffocating silence that envelops us. Behind the officers, I can see the flash of lights outside as the world crowds in around us, and I feel a pang of despair wash over me.

This isn't how our lives were supposed to unfold.

The officers maintain their grip on Oscar, trying to bring him back to rationality, but behind their stern expressions, I see the genuine worry. They can't see me. They can't reach what Oscar and I share.

In his frantic struggles, I reach out, tendrils of earnest love stretching toward him across the vast expanse of nothingness, "Oscar, please! You can't fight this battle alone. I'm still here with you."

But he can't hear me. Each desperate plea only falls further into the abyss. The potent truth grips me, and I fear we will both be lost entirely in this miasma of grief and longing.

Suddenly, perhaps sensing the weight of my eternal presence, Oscar stills, breath hitching as he lifts his head, his eyes darting around, full of a haunted wayward light. A spark of recognition flickers behind the shards of terror. I can feel it.

"Oscar," I whisper, though my voice carries only as a gentle caress in the cavernous void surrounding us. "I'm here.

I'm right here. Please ... please calm down so they don't hurt you."

The whisper seems to slice through the haze surrounding him, and he stares solemnly, right through the chaos and back toward the essence of our bond that sparkles in the air—nearly tangible.

Maybe it's my imagination and he isn't perceiving my presence at all. I'm honestly not sure. I'm not sure about anything anymore.

The house is swarming with police now. One officer approaches Oscar slowly, his expression not just laced with authority but also tinged with compassion as he lowers his weapon, trying to defuse the situation. "Captain Teague, right?" Oscar nods reluctantly. "We're going to help you. Please cooperate."

"Help?" Oscar scoffs, the tension vibrating in his voice. "I despise that word. Help means leaving my wife alone. Help doesn't mean taking her away from me." His eyes dart desperately around, as though searching for an escape route.

He clings to the idea that I'm still just sleeping peacefully in the other room. I can feel it.

"You're only making things worse for yourself, sir," another officer states, a calm emphasis attempting to pierce the rising confusion and chaos. "We need to talk to you about what happened here."

"No! You don't understand!" Oscar bellows, his frame trembling with unspent energy. "She needs me! She's not dead!"

Each word he shouts hits harder than the last, but I can see the struggle reigning within him.

"Please listen to us, Captain," the gentle officer says again, speaking slowly. "We can help you, but first, you have to help us understand what's going on."

A flicker of uncertainty flashes across Oscar's face. I push my way forward, desperately trying to reach him.

"Oscar!" I call, my voice echoing even in the void. "You have to open your heart to them. They're here to help."

Help. Help. Help.

If only we'd gotten help *before*. When all this could have been prevented. If only I'd tried harder to send an SOS. To convince people that our lives weren't perfect. That we were in real trouble.

He stares at me, unseeing yet somehow sensing my presence, torn between the world of living flesh and these phantoms that surround him. "Sierra ..." he breathes, voice trailing into confusion.

"Turn to them. You need to!" I cry out, but all I see in his eyes is confusion.

One of the officers cautiously advances again, lowering his own voice, calming and sincere. "Captain Teague, the way you're feeling right now—it's okay to feel lost."

I can see the internal battle unfold on Oscar's face as the tears gather, shimmering and blurring. He sways on his feet.

Suddenly, I notice Beth. She's talking to an officer on the front porch, her cheeks wet from crying.

She looks our way, her expression shifting from concern to disbelief. "Oscar," she calls out, voice trembling, "please—just listen to them."

I see the flicker of recognition cross his face again, and it's as if the fragile threads of understanding are beginning to weave through.

"Then help me!" he finally moans. He sounds utterly exhausted. "Just get me out of this."

The officers exchange relieved glances, sensing the shift as they inch closer, ready to offer their hands, their support. "Okay, Captain. We're here for you. Just breathe," one of them says, stepping forward with cautious compassion. "Let's figure this out together. We're not here to hurt you."

I reach out, desperate to fill the air with warmth, to push through the veil that holds us apart. "I'm with you, Oscar." I urge, feeling the energetic tether between us pulsing faintly, frail but undeniably present.

His body relaxes slightly, the fiery resolve softening as he lowers his gaze, staring at the ground beneath his feet with an expression of defeat. "I can't lose her," he whispers.

"You won't lose me," I murmur fervently, though I don't even know if that's true.

I yearn to cross that divide, to embody the love that has always been our anchor.

"Let's get you to a safe space first," the officer says gently, and as they prepare to guide Oscar away from the tumult, I feel as if everything is leveling out just a little, allowing for a flicker of hope.

"Get through this, my love," I whisper, feeling my essence wrap around him even as the fabric of reality pulls at our connection.

As they finally coax him gently away from the house and usher him into the back of a squad car, I watch with bated breath, hoping against hope that maybe—just maybe—this is the first step in finding our way back to one another.

How? I don't know.

I turn my attention to Beth. My friend. This must be hard for her.

She finishes a conversation with the police then pulls her phone out of a pocket. I move closer and look over her shoulder as she searches through old emails. What's she looking for? My spirit sinks when I realize she's looking up my parents' phone number.

Oh, no.

Tearfully, she dials, then puts the call on speakerphone and waits as the phone rings.

"Please don't," I whisper, wishing I could somehow intervene. "You don't need to do this."

But my words drift into the void, unheard and unnoted. The space around me remains static, trapped in a suffocating silence.

"Hi, Mrs. Mallory?" Beth's voice quavers slightly as she continues the call, the familiar warmth cracked by anxiety. "It's Beth Tucker. I'm calling to let you know that ... well, something has happened. I think it's best if you come to Virginia."

I instinctively recoil, hearing the tremor in Beth's voice as she conveys the dreadful news about Oscar and me. I wish I could scream at her to hang up, but I remain powerless—adrift in this spectral limbo, tethered to a reality I can only observe.

"We don't know exactly what happened yet," Beth continues, her voice steadying. "It's just ... when you arrive, maybe authorities will know more."

There's a beat of silence before my mom responds, her voice filled with worry. "Did he do this to her?"

"Um," Beth hesitates, looking toward the police officers

standing by, the concern in her eyes evident as they nod at her, urging her to be candid. "I don't know. But I think he needs help, and I think it's important for you to be here. Arrangements will need to be made."

I can almost hear the rush of tension as my mother processes the words. "We'll be there right away."

The moments that follow are painfully slow as the police officers converse with Beth, their voices layering into the atmosphere as I stand suspended in an uncertain twilight. I want to call out to them, but every time I attempt to cut through the veil, I find it solid and impenetrable. There's a solid barrier holding me back.

As time trudges on, it dawns on me that I haven't yet looked at myself. At my ... dead body.

Reluctantly, I turn my gaze toward the living room. I don't want to look, but something compels me to look. I *have* to look.

There, I see myself—the lifeless form sprawled unceremoniously on the floor, the gentle light cascading over my stillness. My heart, if it were still beating, would shatter. How could this be? The sight strikes a painful chord within me. The terrible sight is a solidification of the reality I wish so fervently weren't true.

I look so peaceful, almost dreamlike. And I look pretty. I'm struck by how beautiful my body is ... or should I say, was? It's as if I'm seeing myself objectively for the first time. I no longer feel critical of my thick thighs, my big nose, or my fuzzy hair. All I see is beauty.

I approach, trembling, realizing that the woman they're holding onto—the flicker of hope Oscar clings to—is gone. There's no going back.

I'm here. Not there.

"Please don't fall apart, Oscar," I whisper, my voice breaking at the edges.

I'm afraid of what will happen if the life we cherished slips through his fingers entirely.

I move closer to my body, desperate to understand. To feel. It's all so disorienting. I sense the ache in my being deepening.

It's a sorrow that transcends mere fatigue.

As I hover helplessly, I catch the glimmer of Beth's form standing by. Her heart is heavy with concern, yet there is a resolve in her posture.

"Stay strong for him, and be kind, okay?" I murmur softly, the words barely escaping my lips.

I want to wrap around her, to infuse her with the love I hold for both her and Oscar, to keep her grounded.

Beth nods, the determination in her eyes reflecting the fiery spirit I admire about her. She may not see me, but she'll guard my memory fiercely. There's a comfort in that truth as I drift closer to her warmth.

"We're going to notify our homicide detective," one of the officers states, nodding toward the door. "CSI will need to do a thorough examination of the premises."

Beth's eyes widen, worry spilling across her features. "Wait, you're not going to take her away yet, are you? Her parents are coming from Savannah. I just spoke to her mom."

The officer hesitates. "That's customary procedure, ma'am. We need to ensure everything is handled properly. The circumstances here warrant further investigation. Her parents can view your friend's body in the morgue."

"No," Beth insists, voice steady but filled with panic.

"Her parents should be here when you move her. Someone should watch over her, you know?"

My heart sinks further at her words. If they touch my body, if they take it away, there's a heaviness in my soul that tells me Oscar won't know how to cope.

"Please help my husband," I implore silently, desperate for a connection that transcends the walls between us.

"Ma'am," the officer says sharply, recognizing Beth's rising distress. "We have protocols we must follow. I'm sorry. You'll need to be questioned, too."

Beth's eyes glisten with frustration and disbelief.

"Okay," she finally says. "Please, take good care of her."

Chapter Twenty

OSCAR

I listen from the back of the squad car as an officer sits in the front seat and converses through his radio.

"Dispatch, this is Unit 421. We are code 3 at 512 Creekwalk Lane," he says. “We have a female victim, 10-54, appears to be deceased. Suspected 187. The husband is on the scene, and we have him 10-15, detained. Requesting additional units and a supervisor on scene, over."

"Copy that, Unit 421. Confirm the suspect is detained?" asks the crackly voice over the speaker.

"Affirmative, dispatch. Suspect is detained. Be advised, the suspect appears mentally unstable. He’s displaying erratic behavior, possibly a 5150 situation. We need a mental health crisis unit and medical personnel on scene, over."

"10-4, Unit 421. Confirming the suspect is 5150—mentally unstable?" comes the reply.

I recognize some of the jargon, but feel distanced from it all. It’s almost as if they’re talking about someone else.

Not Sierra. Not me.

"Affirmative,” the officer says. “The suspect is disoriented, talking to himself, and making incoherent statements. He's not aggressive—at the moment—but seems confused. Requesting mental health evaluation and EMS for a psychiatric assessment, over."

"Copy that," the dispatcher replies. "Additional units, supervisor, and EMS en route. Mental health crisis team notified and will be on site as soon as possible. Is the scene secure?"

"Scene is secure, dispatch. We're keeping the suspect calm, but we'll need assistance with transport. He may require medical sedation, over."

Dispatch doesn't skip a beat. "Understood, Unit 421. Mental health crisis team and EMS are en route with estimated arrival in 5 minutes. Keep us updated on the situation. Do you need anything else?"

"Negative at this time, dispatch. Will await additional units and medical personnel. Unit 421 out."

The officer returns his handset to its holster on the dash, then turns and looks my way. I can't get a read on his feelings toward me. It seems like he's just a guy doing his duty. The rational part of me is okay with that.

The next few hours are a whirlwind of sedatives, questions, and procedures as officers watch me like hawks.

I'm taken to the Woodbridge police station where I'm placed in a dimly lit room with a decent chair. I'm given a bottle of water and a granola bar, then I'm asked about my mental health history. Even in my distraught state of mind, I can tell they're being nice to me. I'm not sure why, but I appreciate it. This could be a lot worse.

Can they tell by looking at me that something is very

wrong? That thought disturbs me more than almost any other. Is that what Sierra saw when she looked at me?

I'm sitting alone, staring at a concrete wall when Dr. Caleb Grenier walks in. An older woman with long white hair is with him, and I get the idea she's there to record our conversation. Perhaps to witness it as well. Both are in civilian clothing. No military or police uniforms.

Dr. Grenier is unassuming, his demeanor calm as he approaches. He's wearing wire-rimmed glasses that sit low on his nose, and he carries a well-worn briefcase.

"Good afternoon, Captain Teague," he says, his voice soft and steady. "My name is Dr. Grenier, and this is Ms. Thompson. We're here to talk with you about what's been going on. For now, I will act as your military liaison."

I nod, the storm of emotions swirling just below the surface. I'm remarkably calm, probably from the sedatives. Perhaps I should have taken some of those a long time ago.

"I don't need to talk," I reply, my voice barely above a whisper. "I just want to go home."

Dr. Grenier takes a seat across from me, his expression unreadable. "I understand this is difficult for you, but I need you to tell me what happened today."

"I don't know," I say. "It all happened so fast. One moment, we were talking about dinner, and then ... then everything just went wrong." I lean back in my chair, staring at the wall. "I yelled. I didn't mean to yell. I'd just had a bad day."

"Making things okay can be quite challenging, especially when emotions run high," Dr. Grenier observes, leaning forward slightly. "Can you talk to me about the feelings that overwhelmed you?"

When I don't respond, he continues gently. "It's important to express how you feel, especially after such a traumatic experience."

I frown, struggling to articulate the chaos that has become my life. "There was this guy. At the gas station. I lost control, and I don't even know why. But it felt good," I admit, the words spilling out before I can stop myself. "Too good. Like maybe I wanted to feel something—anything—but anger."

"That's understandable," Dr. Grenier remarks, jotting quick notes. "Sometimes we lash out when we don't know how to express confusion or grief. What happened after that?"

"I came home, and things didn't feel right. I thought I'd just pretend everything was normal. I tried, but ... it's like the moment I opened the door, the weight of the world crashed down on me. I—I can't lose her," I confess, choking on the last words. "I love my wife dearly."

Dr. Grenier nods, his expression calm yet attentive. "It sounds like you're carrying an immense burden. Can you tell me more about your wife? Sierra Mallory?"

"I can't lose her," I repeat, desperation creeping into my voice. "She's everything to me. I wanted to make things perfect, to fix everything and put it all back together again. But I kept pretending, and I hurt her. I tried to connect, but how do you fix something that feels so broken?"

Ms. Thompson, the woman seated beside Dr. Grenier, looks up, her pen hovering above her notepad. Maybe I'm imagining it, but her eyes seem to reflect understanding. I find it oddly comforting.

"I want to help you work through this, Oscar," Dr.

Grenier urges gently. "But we need to unpack what's been happening. It sounds like you've been under significant stress, especially after the helicopter you were riding in crashed. I read about the accident in your file that General Benedict provided."

"Stress? This isn't just stress!" I exclaim, the walls closing in once again. "This is losing myself. I thought everything would go back to normal, but it hasn't. I don't even know who I am anymore. I don't know what happened to Sierra."

"Identity loss can be a profound experience, especially in challenging moments," Dr. Grenier observes, his tone measured. "Perhaps focusing on what you do recognize about yourself might help. What did you love about your life before all this?"

I shake my head, frustration bubbling up. "I don't know. It feels like all the things that defined me—my love for Sierra, the joy in serving my country, the laughter, it's like they're all just shadows now. I used to be a fun guy. I had friends. I never got in trouble at work or with the law. Not once. I even had a dog once—a German shepherd named Hugo. I'd planned to surprise Sierra with a puppy, but ... All I have left is this emptiness."

There's a silence as Dr. Grenier absorbs my words, giving me space to breathe. "Did you speak with Sierra about how you feel?"

I feel my breath hitch, regret washing over me like a tidal wave. "I tried, but not well enough. She deserves someone stronger, someone who can protect her. I don't know if I can be that man anymore."

"Your wife loves you regardless of these struggles," Dr. Grenier replies, his voice steady. "It's important to remember that vulnerability can bring strength in connection. Can you share your feelings with her when you see her next?"

My heart sinks at the thought. "If I see her again."

"Why wouldn't you?" he asks gently.

"What if I've lost her for good?" I whisper, the world around me dimming in anguish.

The room lingers in silence. Dr. Grenier shifts forward slightly, his expression unwavering. He's gauging my reaction.

"I know it feels overwhelming right now, Oscar, but there is always hope," he encourages. "People come back from the brink. It's a matter of finding the right support and allowing yourself to be vulnerable enough to reach out."

"I don't know how to do that," I confess, my voice cracking under the immense pressure of my emotions. "How do I even begin to face something like this?"

"By taking small steps," he replies, his tone calm. "Recognizing what you feel and allowing space for those emotions without fear of judgment. It's important to grasp that failure or fear doesn't define your worth."

"I don't even think I can face Sierra if I don't know what to say," I admit, burying my head in my hands. "I can't let her see me like this. I failed her."

He has quite the poker face. I recognize this much even though my grip on reality is feeble. Is he trying to coax something out of me? A confession?

"In these moments of darkness, Oscar, it's essential to realize that reaching out, regardless of your state, can bridge the gap of isolation you're feeling," Dr. Grenier says, his voice warm and steady. "The most profound healing often comes from acknowledging our vulnerabilities in front of those we love."

“But what if she’s angry?” I can barely hold back the bittersweet tears pooling in my eyes. “What if I’ve hurt her beyond measure?”

“Ask her, Oscar,” the doctor implores softly. “Confront those fears directly. Give her the opportunity to share her own thoughts and feelings, the way you’ve tried to.”

“What if she’s gone?” I burst out, the pain lacing through my words heavy like iron chains. “What if I never get that chance?”

Dr. Grenier leans back, allowing the question to linger in the air for a long moment. “That is a possibility, yes. But in the face of uncertainty, what’s important is that you allow yourself to feel those emotions and express them. Emphasis on ‘express.’ Often it’s the expression that leads to healing.”

I nod, disheartened but realizing there’s truth in his words. “I don’t know if I have the strength to do that.”

“You do,” he reassures me. “Finding strength even in your weakest moments is key. And when you find that strength, you can begin to confront what’s haunting you.”

He leans back, pulling an old-fashioned prescription pad out of his pocket. Ms. Thompson nods, as if she's been waiting for this part. "I'm going to prescribe something to help you begin to feel more like yourself. You'll take one right away, then I'll need you to come to the medical center for a series of tests, first thing tomorrow morning."

The thought of going back home right now makes me physically ill. Dr. Grenier seems to see that, so he explains further.

"You'll be spending the night here, at the police station. I'll be frank with you, Captain Teague. You're going to be arrested and booked. I know it will be unpleasant, but I want you to have faith that I will get to the bottom of what's happening in your head. Once I do, the authorities will receive all of the findings and medical records they need to handle your case accordingly."

I stare at him with a mix of shock and disbelief. I don't know how to process this.

"Why couldn't you have helped me a week ago? Or a month ago?"

He returns my eye contact. "I'm sorry, Captain. I wish I had. Your situation was just brought to my attention this afternoon ... probably around the same hour of the incident at your home. The timing is ... unfortunate."

"Unfortunate? That's an understatement," I mutter. "I've probably lost my wife, and now I'm being told I'm going to jail."

"This is standard procedure, given the circumstances. I'll be here for you through this. It's easy to feel isolated right now, but I promise you, you'll have access to treatment throughout the process."

I scoff bitterly, the taste of my own misery too familiar. "Treatment for what? I barely even recognize myself anymore."

"I don't know yet," he replies gently. "But we'll figure it out. Acknowledging something is wrong is the most profound act of strength. Today might feel like an ending, but it can also be a beginning if you let it. You'll have the opportunity to heal and rebuild, while also learning more about how to maintain your mental health long-term."

"It all feels so pointless," I rasp, holding onto that bitter edge feeling. "What if I can't fix this? What if Sierra never wakes up? I can't lose her. If I do, then nothing matters anymore."

Dr. Grenier's response is careful, measured. "And if she does wake up?" he asks, narrowing his eyes slightly. "Have you thought about how you will face her? That's why working through this—understanding yourself—is so paramount. You've had a tumultuous experience, but that doesn't define your future. You can learn to communicate better and manage the pain you're feeling right now. With time and effort, you can rebuild those aspects of yourself."

I take a shaky breath, his words settling back into the depths of my heart. "What if I never get the chance to show her?" I murmur, feeling the despair creeping back in. "What if by the time I'm ready, she's already ..."

"Then you fight for your rights and her memory," he interjects firmly, glancing toward Ms. Thompson. "The process of healing is rarely linear. You will have setbacks, but that doesn't mean you won't make progress. Fights worth fighting take time."

Chapter Twenty-One

SIERRA

Time has bent and morphed for me, but I hear an officer at the police station say that it's after midnight when my parents arrive. They must have gotten in the car immediately and driven straight through.

I somehow followed Oscar here from our house. I can't explain how the transport happened, but I sat near him in the back seat of a patrol car and stuck close. Now I'm here, watching and listening.

Mom and Dad look haggard when they walk through the front doors. I feel a pang of deep sadness when I see their pained expressions.

"Hi, I'm Jennifer Mallory and this is my husband Marty Mallory," Mom says to the officer manning the front desk. "We're here about our daughter ..."

She bursts into tears, unable to finish the sentence.

The officer watches them carefully, sympathy etched on his face as he gestures for them to sit in the waiting area. "We understand this is difficult. A detective will be with you shortly."

Still hovering, I feel an overwhelming need to comfort them, but I can do nothing. I'm just a specter caught in this bleak limbo. I can sense the dread that looms over the room—my parents' anguish palpable—and it pierces through me like a knife.

My mother wipes her eyes with trembling hands, a soft resolve starting to spread across her features. "We need to talk to Oscar," she whispers, her voice edged with a desperate clarity. "Is he okay? Where is he?"

The officer nods slowly. "He's in a separate area for his protection and processing. You'll have a chance to see him shortly, but I need to let you know that it's not going to be easy. There was a confrontation at your home earlier today, and there are some pressing concerns regarding his mental state."

"Concerns?" Dad marvels, disbelief cutting through his voice. "What do you mean? What happened?"

The officer exchanges a glance with another officer nearby and then resumes, "The situation escalated. He was distressed, and there were some allegations of violence."

"Violence?" Mom asks.

My heart sinks further, contemplating the worst and imagining the feelings that must have surged through Oscar, knowing he was losing everything.

This was a terrible accident. Nothing more.

"I don't know the details, ma'am, but I'm afraid I can't share much until you speak with the detective," he says, his tone kind but firm.

Mom turns away, a look of dread filling her eyes. "I need to see Oscar Teague. Right now."

"We'll arrange that for you," the officer assures them, but

his gaze reveals that he understands—this won't be easy. He escorts them to a private room, then exits and closes the door.

The minutes stretch on with agonizing slowness as we all wait. My parents fidget, wordlessly attempting to rally their strength while I float in sorrowful silence. I wish Beth was here to comfort them.

Then I see him.

Oscar is led into the room by two officers. He looks disheveled and lost, his face shadowed with confusion. I catch the glimpses of raw anger still lingering in the depths of his eyes. For a split second, I want to call out to him, to leap over the physical and metaphysical divide and hold him tight.

"Oscar!"

All I can do is watch as he moves toward my parents, the space between them dense with unspoken questions and sharp, unyielding emotions. He stands before them, shifting from foot to foot, clearly lost, and I feel a wave of sorrow wash over me.

My husband looks like a little boy about to be scolded for bad behavior. Not a decorated Marine Corps Captain with a stellar record and reputation.

It's dreadfully sad.

"Mr. and Mrs. Mallory," one officer begins, clearing his throat. "Captain Teague has been placed under detention for his own safety and for further assessment regarding today's events."

"Events?" Dad repeats, thick with disbelief. "What happened? Where's Sierra?"

Oscar's expression falters, the light that once sparkled with love and warmth now dulled by confusion and despair. "She's ... she's fine. She's just sleeping," he says, voice strained.

How long is he going to keep telling himself that?

"No, she's not," Mom interjects. "She's not fine. You need to tell us the truth about what's going on."

My soul aches with the weight of her words.

"It's not what you think," Oscar mutters, biting his lip with strained determination. "I didn't mean to hurt her. I was just angry, and it all got out of control. I thought she might—"

"Thought she might what?" Dad cuts in, a mix of anger and concern racing through his voice. "You don't understand what's at stake here, do you? You pushed her or shoved her or whatever you did to her, and she's lying ... somewhere. She's dead, Oscar. She isn't coming back."

I feel the tension crackle between them, an energy that elevates my sorrow, and I want to scream—not out of anger but pure heartbreak.

This isn't the reunion I wanted. This isn't what I envisioned for us.

"Where is she?" Oscar wails, tears finally spilling down his cheeks. "I need her! I can't do this without her!"

"It's okay," Mom murmurs, reaching out instinctively to comfort him. Her maternal instinct rises to the fore, even as Dad shoots her a perplexed look. "We're here now. We'll handle things."

"Let us talk to the professionals," Dad implores in a calm but firm tone, struggling to contain his emotions. "They'll know how to help. But we'll need you to be honest about what happened today."

Oscar nods slowly, the fight trickling away from him as he swipes at his tears. "If I could only tell her I'm sorry," he chokes out. "I didn't mean to hurt her. I wasn't in control of myself."

Mom reaches forward, her hands grasping his. "You need to let them help you, Oscar. This is a serious situation. You're sick."

"I know," he whispers, his voice barely audible, but I can see the fear in his eyes. "I need her back. I didn't take care of her like I should have."

The world around me thickens as their words hang in the air, filled with a growing tension and sorrow. I yearn to reach him, to wrap my love around him like a shield against the despair threatening to pull him under. "I'm still here, Oscar. Please don't lose hope," I beg silently, but he cannot hear me.

"Detective Richards is on his way to speak with you," the officer interjects, breaking the silence. "He'll have some more questions about what transpired."

"More questions? I'll try," Oscar replies, exhaustion etched deep into his features. The weight of it all threatens to crush him, and I feel that familiar ache—as much as I want to reach out and comfort him, I am still caught in this hazy limbo.

This is brutal.

The door to the room creaks open again, and Detective Richards steps in, his presence commanding immediate attention. He's Asian with a neat haircut and muscular build. I suspect he's former military. That's helpful. Maybe he and Oscar will get along.

"Good evening," the detective says, his tone professional yet imbued with a sincere concern. "I apologize for the circumstances bringing us together tonight."

Oscar straightens his back, a mixture of fear and stubbornness flickering in his eyes. “You’re not taking her away, are you?”

The detective raises a hand and shakes his head slowly. “Let's remain calm. We’re here to understand the situation. I need to begin with your account of events today.”

Oscar swallows hard, his throat constricting as I can almost see the memories pull at him like chains, tightening around his heart. “I already told the other cops."

"Tell me again."

Oscar sighs. "I didn’t mean to hurt her. I just lost control. I thought ... I thought everything would go back to normal,” he stammers, desperation bleeding through each word.

Detective Richards nods patiently, indicating with a gesture for him to continue. “Can you tell me what led up to that moment? What was going on before the incident?”

“Sierra and I were arguing,” Oscar breathes, pain etching deeper lines on his face. “I was angry. She tried to reach me. I just ... none of it made sense. I wanted to fix things, but I didn’t know how.”

“Take your time, Captain,” the detective urges, his gaze unwavering. “I need to understand exactly what happened. Let’s start from the beginning.”

I feel the tension in Oscar’s posture loosen just slightly, as if the detective's calm demeanor is giving him the courage to face the memories. He nods, closing his eyes briefly as he collects himself.

“We were at home,” he begins, voice trembling. “I was struggling, frustrated with everything going on. Sierra was worried about me. It felt like she was trying to control me. I thought I could just ignore how I felt, that I could shove it all down, but it built up until it exploded.”

I can sense my parents hanging on every word, their eyes wide with concern. This is probably their worst nightmare. I hate to see them going through this. Absolutely hate it.

"It escalated," Oscar continues, tears glistening in his eyes as he looks away. "I yelled. I said things I didn't mean, and then ..." His voice breaks. "Then it just happened. I didn't intend for her to get hurt. I don't even remember exactly how it happened. I don't even know for sure *what* happened. I just got angry and scared, and everything spiraled out of control."

Detective Richards takes a step closer. "Captain, it's important that you understand the consequences are grave. You need to own your actions and the impact they had."

"I know," Oscar whispers, his voice cracking with emotion. "But I never meant for it to get to this point. I thought she was just tired, you know? I thought if I let her sleep it off, everything would be fine."

Detective Richards nods, maintaining eye contact to keep Oscar anchored. "But it isn't fine, Captain."

Oscar shakes his head, defeated. "I keep thinking if I'd just been stronger ... if I'd just controlled myself better ..."

Suddenly, Dad stands. "I can't take this," he says, biting back tears. "Our little girl ... Please, question him somewhere else."

Mom nods her agreement.

This is gut wrenching to watch.

"I'm so tired," Oscar says. "Tired of fighting, tired of pretending. I'm terrified of what I've become."

Oscar does look groggy, like he desperately needs to sleep. Maybe he's drugged. I saw them give him a sedative earlier.

"Okay, that's enough for now," the detective says. He

motions to a guard outside the door who steps in and escorts Oscar out.

As my husband stands, just before he leaves the room, he looks at my parents regretfully. "I'm sorry."

With that, Oscar is led out of the room and a heavy silence settles over us, punctuated only by the ticking of a clock on the wall. Time itself feels as if it's grinding to a halt.

Just like that, though, I feel my own tether starting to fray.

The sensation is akin to being pulled from a warm embrace into frigid waters.

I follow Oscar and yearn to reach out to him, to tell him that I understand—even if he can't see me, doesn't know I'm still here, caught in this silly limbo between life and death. I watch helplessly as he moves further away, the shadows wrapping around him as the officers lead him through the maze of the police station, taking him out of my sight. I try, but I can't keep up.

Movement in this form is tricky. I haven't mastered it yet.

"Where is she?" I can almost hear him ask, the fear visible on his face.

"Just breathe," the officers murmur, their voices barely audible to me now as they guide him further from the room.

Suddenly, I'm overwhelmed by the wave of despair crashing within me. My soul aches with desperate longing. It hurts so much.

"Mom, Dad," I whisper, my voice cracking as I float back to my parents who remain seated, shock still painting their features. "I'm here. Please don't give up on him."

I want so desperately to comfort them, to wrap the love I

hold for both of them around their shoulders, but my essence shifts, flickering like a candle at the mercy of the wind.

They sit together, shoulders hunched over, tears glistening on their cheeks as the reality of what's happening sinks further in. I can feel their worry. It's an echo of my own ache. A trembling love that reaches out for me.

"Why?" Mom whispers, her voice laced with anguish. "Why did this happen?"

It strikes me as deep and painful confirmation of what we're all facing, the shattering reality that reverberates with every breath they take. The weight lingers, pulling at the tether of my spirit, squeezing around a heart that can't beat anymore.

Each passing moment draws me deeper into my sorrow, clawing at the remnants of my identity. I want to bring hope back into our lives, but I don't know how to break the cycle of despair that encircles us.

I hover near them, my presence a gentle draft in the still air of the room. "I'm still here. I'm not gone ... I'm not gone," I whisper, my voice wavering between worlds.

The moments feel like an eternity as they remain lost in their thoughts, eyes clouded with unshed tears, contemplating the sadness.

I stay near them as they're taken to a morgue and shown my body. They sputter and gasp at the sight of me. Mom loses her footing and collapses into Dad's arms.

This is torture. The worst day of my life.

Where do we go from here?

PART THREE
Collateral Damage

Chapter Twenty-Two

OSCAR

Eight Months Later

I'm nervous as I button up my uniform. It's been months since I've worn anything but an orange jumpsuit, let alone my dress blues. I asked for permission from the court to wear the uniform, and that permission was granted. I hope the gesture is seen as a sign of respect and pride in my military service. The last thing I want to do is to anger the judge or the members of the jury.

"Captain Teague, they're ready for you," a guard says as he slides the metal door of my cell open. I smooth my short hair, freshly cut for the occasion, then step out into the light.

"Here goes nothing," I say to myself.

I'm loaded into a transport van and taken to the local courthouse.

The trip feels surreal, like a dream where everything is just slightly off. I can see the familiar streets of Woodbridge passing by, the neighborhood I once called home. Now it feels alien, a ghost of a life I can barely reach. Thoughts race in my mind, spinning wildly as I try to prepare for the decision that will unfold today—my fate, and more importantly, the truth of my actions.

As the van rolls to a stop, I'm escorted through the hallways of the courthouse, flanked by guards who keep an eye on me, their expressions unreadable. I clench my jaw, forcing myself to breathe evenly despite the anxiety coursing through my veins.

I'm led into a brightly lit courtroom filled with the weight of expectation. I take a deep breath, trying to still the storm inside. As I step into the room, I catch sight of Sierra's parents and Beth sitting together, their faces etched with concern and love instead of disappointment or anger. It's a sight that fills me with both gratitude and sadness.

Have they forgiven me? Was this all a terrible accident?

I'm still not certain.

I wish more than anything that I could reach out, but the invisible barrier that separates me from them remains, a painful reminder of the distance created by my actions.

A lot has happened in the past eight months. True to his word, Dr. Grenier got to the bottom of what was wrong with me.

As it turns out, I suffer from a neurological condition called Frontal Lobe Syndrome. It's caused by damage to the frontal lobe of the brain, which can occur due to trauma, such as a head injury sustained during a helicopter crash. I take a handful of medications each day, and I'm in therapy with both Dr. Grenier and a colleague of his named Dr. Rashid.

They tell me there's hope for the future, but I'm not so sure. I still get angry and fly into blind rages. They adjust my medications when that happens, but I'm usually just left feeling numb and distant. A mere shell of my former self.

I've come to understand that the Marine Corps didn't do anything to me. There were no secret experiments. No torture or nefarious courses of action. It was the helicopter crash. Simple as that. Everything else was my paranoia talking. My brain playing tricks on me as a result of my injury and resulting condition.

Sierra seemed to know.

She might not have known what to call it, but she knew I wasn't myself. She tried to get help for me. She wanted the best. Wherever she is, I'm sure she still does.

So much depends on what happens here today.

The jury sits silently, their expressions guarded, and the weight of their stares hangs heavily in the air. I can feel the eyes of the prosecution bore into me, searching for weakness, ready to expose my imperfections. Meanwhile, the defense attorney stands and prepares to speak on my behalf. He's a man I've only just begun to trust.

A familiar dread wells up inside me as I take my seat at the defendant's table, and memories of that fateful day crash over me. I close my eyes for a moment, allowing myself to revisit the chaos—the arguments, the anger, the shattering pain as everything spiraled out of control.

There are still gaps in my understanding. Portions of that afternoon I can't recall.

What I do know, for sure, is that Sierra is dead. She's never coming back, and it kills me. Life will never, ever be the same without the love of my life. The devastation can't be put into words.

The judge enters, her voice cutting through the air with authority. "Will the defendant please rise?"

I follow her instructions, standing stiffly in front of the court. "Captain Oscar Teague, you stand before this court today charged with a number of allegations stemming from the incident concerning the death of your wife, Sierra Mallory. How do you plead?"

My throat tightens. "Not guilty, Your Honor." The words taste bitter on my tongue, echoing hollowly against the walls of this room.

"Very well," she replies, a mix of professionalism and understanding flashing in her eyes.

The judge's gaze sweeps over the courtroom, her expression transitioning to an empathetic resolve. "This court acknowledges the gravity of this matter. The implications of what you are accused of weigh heavily not only on you but also on the family affected by this tragic loss. We shall proceed with the testimonies."

The air thickens as I nod, steeling myself against the surge of emotions crashing around me like waves against a rocky shore. My heart races, each tick of the clock echoing in my ears as I prepare for what's to come. Guilt hangs over me now more than ever, and the thought of facing everyone—my wife's parents, my colleagues, the jury—fills me with an overwhelming cocktail of dread and shame.

The prosecution starts its case, laying out an account of the events that led to that fateful day. My heart sinks as they recount the arguments, the tension, my fury. It sounds worse when it's said aloud. Every accusation strikes me like punches to the gut. I can feel the eyes of the jury boring into me, each piercing look amplifying the guilt clawing at my insides.

I catch a glimpse of General Benedict sitting a few rows back. His presence, too, fills me with sadness. The general is a good man. He tried to talk some sense into me. More importantly, he tried to help my wife. He heard her pleas. Only it was already too late.

I remember most of that afternoon vividly—how emotions erupted like a tempest, blurring all rationality as anger coursed through me. But the defense attorney is quick to counter the prosecution's claims, shifting the focus to my mental state—shedding light on the trauma I sustained during the helicopter crash and how it affected my perceptions and judgments.

"Captain Teague is not a man devoid of feelings or love," my attorney asserts, his voice steady. "He was deeply affected by his injuries—a reality acknowledged not just by his doctors, but by all who know him. This is a man who loved his wife deeply. The accident turned him into a shadow of himself as he battled unseen demons."

As he speaks, the words feel like an anchor in my storm. They're a reminder of how much I had once cherished Sierra, and how desperately I had fought to keep her close, even as my mind unraveled into confusion.

That feeling of strength falters when I catch sight of her dad's quivering lip.

Before long, I'm put on the stand and sworn in. Maybe it's foolish to speak about this, but it feels like the right thing to do.

"Do you remember the last conversation you had with your wife?" my attorney prompts gently.

I swallow hard and nod, the memory fresh and painful. "I remember yelling. I remember being so angry," I admit, my voice trembling. “But I also remember the way she looked at me. It was like she was trying to see beyond the confusion, trying to pull me back into the light. I didn’t recognize it then, but she wanted to reach me. To help. I didn’t let her.”

The words spill out as if the dam built around my heart is finally crumbling, and I can no longer suppress the pain I’ve held at bay for far too long.

“I didn’t mean to hurt her,” I choke out, anguish welling in my chest. “I wanted to defend her, but I couldn’t separate the anger I felt from the love I had for her. It was all muddled.”

I still have trouble finding words sometimes, but thankfully, they’re coming to me today.

“Captain Teague,” my attorney says gently, “what were the circumstances leading up to that moment? Were you aware of any changes in your mental state?”

“I was struggling,” I admit. “The helicopter crash in Afghanistan changed everything for me. My thoughts would spiral, and the anger became overwhelming. I felt like I was losing control of who I was. Losing pieces of myself. Sierra was the one person who always kept me grounded, and I didn’t know how to handle it.”

“Could you describe what it felt like to lose your grip?” the attorney urges softly.

“It felt like ... drowning,” I confess, my voice barely above a whisper. “I could see the surface, all the things that made life beautiful—my wife, our laughter, our plans—but that surface kept slipping away from me, and I panicked. I never wanted her to be scared of me. I wanted to protect her, but I couldn’t find the words.”

The memories claw at my heart, and I can’t hold back the

tears any longer. They spill down my cheeks. "She called me her hero once," I murmur, voice breaking. "I never understood how much she needed me to be that hero."

The courtroom is silent as my confession lingers in the heavy air, an emotional weight that transcends the accusations thrown my way. I glance toward Sierra's parents. Their faces remain a mix of heartbreak and understanding.

It's complicated.

"What do you want the jury to understand about your relationship with your wife?" my attorney prompts delicately.

"She was my heart," I say, the truth pouring from my soul. "And I've spent every moment since that day trying to piece together how I lost her. I loved her more than I can express. All the anger that day was a mask, hiding the real fight happening inside me."

As I speak, I can feel the energy shift in the room; the tension eases just slightly, and I see the glimmers of understanding in the eyes of the jury. Perhaps they begin to see me not as an unfeeling monster but a man trapped in the clutches of his own brokenness. A man who loved deeply, fiercely, and yet failed in the most tragic of ways.

"I want you all to know that if I could take it back, I would do anything to have that day over again," I continue. "I would change my response, change my actions, and embrace her through the chaos rather than push her away. I wish I'd listened more and understood her concern better. I wish I hadn't let the darkness win."

The silence that follows is heavy, thick with emotion, and I realize that the apology I've longed to express is finally being heard.

Suddenly, the door creaks open, and a figure steps into

the courtroom. It's Detective Richards. He wears a solemn expression, and I can see the heaviness in his eyes as he approaches the judge. He leans in and whispers something that I can't hear, but I can sense the gravity of the moment.

The judge nods, her demeanor shifting. "Ladies and gentlemen of the jury, we are requesting a brief recess. We have been informed of some developments."

As the gavel strikes down, I feel my heart drop. What could this mean? My palms sweat as I look across the room. Everyone is watching, and I can feel the burden of their expectations weighing on my shoulders.

The courtroom begins to empty, murmurs of confusion swirling around me, and I can't shake the feeling that everything is about to change again.

I take a deep breath, forcing myself to remain steady. The attorney leans in, his voice low but firm. "Hang in there, Captain. We'll regroup soon."

As the conversations ebb and flow around me, I can't shake the sense that something is shifting, a storm brewing just beyond the horizon.

And then I hear it—a voice calling me, resonating deep within the caverns of my heart. "Oscar."

I jerk my head, staring into the crowd, expecting to see an illusion, just a piece of my fractured psyche manifesting the ghost of the woman I've lost. I see her parents, I see the jurors, but none of them is Sierra.

I close my eyes, knees shaking slightly. "Please, come back to me," I breathe, wishing with every fiber of my being that my love could hear me.

But the moment is fleeting, like an illusion. When I open my eyes, the vision is gone.

I turn back to the defense attorney, breathing hard. "What now?" I whisper, fear creeping into my voice. "What are they going to tell us?"

He opens his mouth to respond, but Detective Richards steps forward, having returned to the room with purpose in his stride. "Captain Teague," he says, and his serious tone stops me cold. "We need to discuss something important. Can we step outside for a moment?"

My gut tightens. "What's going on? Is this about Sierra?"

The detective hesitates, his gaze shifting as he chooses his words cautiously, probably gauging the weight of what he's carrying. "It's about Sierra's case and some new developments that have come to light."

My heart races, uncertainty flooding my mind. "Is she—? I mean, do you have news about her?"

His expression softens slightly, but there's an underlying gravity in his eyes. "Let's talk outside."

Panic surges as I nod dumbly, allowing the detective to guide me out of the courtroom and into the cool corridor beyond. I can feel the weight of every decision pressing on me —the fear of the unknown and the desperation for any shred of news, any glimmer of hope.

"Just breathe," he says, his voice steady, as if sensing the tumult inside me. "I know this is hard. We're navigating a complicated situation, but I need you to focus."

Once in the corridor, the weight of the world feels even heavier, the reality of the day slowly sinking in. The other officers stand watch at varying distances, discreetly observing my every move.

"Detective, please," I urge, struggling against the rising tide of anxiety, "what's happened?"

Detective Richards stops, allowing the gravity of my plea to linger in the air. "We've received word from the medical examiner," he starts, his voice low, filled with unsealed concern. "There are some complications surrounding Sierra's case that we need to address."

I feel my stomach churn. "Complications? What do you mean?"

Chapter Twenty-Three

SIERRA

I'd like to say that things have changed for me. That I've been bestowed with some cosmic understanding of the meaning of life and am now living happily in eternal bliss.

That's not the case.

Instead, I still hang around, stuck to this reality like it's a curse. I suspect something went wrong with the dying process. Or, more likely, that I'm waiting on something. I wish I knew what. This existence is not what I wish for myself.

I mostly follow Oscar around in his cell. He doesn't leave it much. Sometimes, I go to my parents or to Beth. I've even hung out with Carl and Dr. Singh a time or two. I am getting better at moving myself from place to place, but it's little consolation when I'm stuck in this dreary realm. It's a crying shame that I'm, apparently, destined to live every day with my earthly friends and family, yet I have no way to communicate with them.

Maybe I'm waiting for Oscar to grow old and die, too.

Then we could be together again. He'd be free of the brain condition we've now learned about. Our love could be unburdened once more.

That would be nice.

Speaking of the Frontal Lobe Syndrome, I knew it. That diagnosis explains everything. Understanding why Oscar's behavior changed so dramatically proves what I said all along —he couldn't help it and it wasn't his fault.

The poor guy.

Today, I linger in the cloudy haze of the courtroom, feeling the tremors of emotion pulse through the air as the trial continues to unfold like a tapestry woven with pain. As witnesses relay their testimony, a weight settles heavily on my being. It overshadows the memories of laughter and love that have kept me grounded all this time.

Sifting through the details of what happened is a grueling process, for everyone involved.

I float quietly, a silent observer in a world where no one can see me. My heart—a heart that no longer beats—aches when I hear the words echo through the chambers of justice, words that speak of responsibility, choices, and consequences. The consequences of Oscar's actions begin to crystallize in my mind, and the more I listen to the testimonies, the more the truth reveals itself.

I'd convinced myself that it wasn't his fault. That it was merely an accident. A result of the injuries he endured in that disastrous helicopter crash. That he didn't strike or push me. That I simply fell in the middle of the commotion, then hit my head.

As the fragments of the trial weave together, clarity begins to penetrate the fog.

Was my husband responsible for my untimely death? That's the question the judge and jury have come here to answer.

"Captain Teague lost control of his emotions," the prosecution argues with steely precision, detailing how anger turned to violence and how heated words spiraled out of control, leading up to that fateful moment. "This wasn't merely self-defense. It wasn't an accident. It was a manifestation of rage, a tempest that ultimately cost a life."

I shiver, the chill of it running through me as the sharp reality sinks deeper.

Sierra Mallory is gone.

I am gone.

In the aftermath, the arguments, confessions, and stories of relationships unraveling batter away at the walls of denial I've built. Each depiction of that day pulls me closer to the truth I'd been resisting since the moment the world slipped away from me.

"I—I didn't mean to hurt her!" Oscar's voice rings out, heavy with despair as he recalls that moment of unfiltered fury. "I lost control. She was everything to me."

The feeling of tears falling from my eyes overwhelms me. I can't actually cry, but the feeling is almost the same.

Rooted in sorrow, I float closer to Oscar, still wishing to wrap him in the warmth of my love. To tell him that it's okay. That he can find me on the other side of this tragedy.

"I was scared. I thought I was going to lose her." he admits, and there's a vulnerability in his expression that cuts deep.

I'm torn. How can I comfort him if I know the truth? The truth that my death was a consequence of his unchecked rage. An explosion of darkness that shattered the very foundation of our love. It's not just about losing him. It's about the reality that he *was* responsible.

I take a step back, letting the weight of the truth settle over me. I've been clinging to the notion that this was purely an accident. A tragic twist of fate. I fell. But deep down, I have to acknowledge the reality that my existence hangs in the balance of Oscar's choices.

That's not right, and it's not fair.

With every testimony, with every piercing look from the jury, it becomes painfully clear. To stay spiritually tethered to Oscar might just keep me locked in this endless cycle of pain. And yet, how do I separate myself from the man I loved with every fiber of my being?

I watch as he breaks down. "I can't live with this," he repeats, voice cracking. "She was my light. My everything. I didn't want to lose her, but I didn't know what I was doing."

The tears stream down his face unabated as I hover close by, torn between the fierce love I once had for him and the truth that now extends like a chasm between us. I want to comfort him, to tell him that I'm still in his heart. Yet I also feel the sharp pull of my own grief. It's a scream locked in a throat that can no longer project sound.

"Your Honor," the prosecutor presses on, turning toward the jury, their faces void of sympathy. "This wasn't just a tragic loss. It was preventable. Captain Teague's actions had dire consequences, and it's time for him to face those consequences."

The weight of accountability hangs like an iron anchor as I listen. He loved me, yes, but love isn't always enough. In the quiet that fills the courtroom as the prosecution rests, I sense my own spirit wavering.

What do I want? Where do I stand in all of this?

Sierra Mallory is gone, but what I create from this experience—what I choose to carry forward—still lies within my grasp.

I must decide whether I cling to our love's legacy or set myself free from the chains of Oscar's tumultuous despair. Deep down, I knew it was in him long before any of this. The crash didn't create it from nothing. It exasperated what already existed somewhere. Not to say it's Oscar's fault, exactly, but it certainly isn't mine.

Why should I suffer along with him? Why should I be okay with paying the ultimate price?

As the defense rises to present its case, I watch Oscar's expression shift from one of raw anguish to fragile hope. "I can do better," he says softly, looking toward the judge. "I want to make amends for what I've done. I never wanted this."

The defense attorney begins to lay the groundwork for Oscar's case, discussing his struggles, the psychological trauma stemming from the crash, and the path he's undertaken to heal. "Captain Teague is willing to commit to therapy and community service," he stresses, his voice ringing with truth. "He understands the gravity of his choices and wishes to honor Sierra's memory by giving back."

The jury listens intently, some appearing empathetic, while others remain skeptical. This is their chance to get a glimpse beneath the surface.

I don't wish for him to suffer.

"I want to be better," Oscar tells my parents, sincerity

flooding his gaze. “Sierra was everything to me, and I know I can’t change what happened, but I refuse to let her memory fade. I want to honor her by being the man she loved.”

His words cut through the air. They’re raw, unfiltered, and overwhelming.

After a brief recess where Detective Richards speaks with Oscar outside in the hall, they return and the judge calls the court back to order. The courtroom holds its collective breath as the detective steps forward.

I'm nervous as I catch a glimpse of his expressions, knowing he carries significant news. I suspect it’s a revelation that could tip the balance of everything I’ve been trying to piece back together.

"Your Honor, I have just been informed about new evidence concerning this case," Detective Richards states firmly, drawing every eye in the room. There's a mixture of tension and unease as all attention turns to him.

“What kind of evidence?” the judge asks.

Detective Richards glances briefly at the jury, then back at Oscar. “We have further information regarding the events leading to the tragic death of Sierra Mallory.”

My spirit drops at the sound of my own name.

“A second opinion analysis of the autopsy report has revealed crucial details,” the detective continues, his voice strong and steady. “It confirms that there were injuries consistent with an altercation, but there's more. Dr. Mallory’s death was indeed a result of blunt force trauma, and not just from the corner of the coffee table.”

Fury erupts within me, twisting up from my gut. I can feel Oscar’s anguish spilling over.

"No," he whispers in disbelief. "No, that can't be true. I didn't hurt her! I didn't mean to hurt her!"

I want to reach out. I want to tell him that we can get through this together, but the truth is hanging in the room, a palpable force. It's becoming crystal clear that I've denied the depths of what happened.

Detective Richards presses on. "We have a witness statement. An account from a neighbor who observed the confrontation through the window. A pattern has emerged. We believe this was not merely an incident in isolation. There were arguments leading up to this moment that indicated something deeper," he states, not faltering.

"No!" Oscar cries.

The echoes of Oscar's words claw at my heart, but they no longer feel like the lifeline I once treasured. My sense of connection to him is frayed.

"I have an expert who will testify that Captain Teague struck his wife before she fell. Marks on the captain's hands and evidence on the scene suggest that the confrontation was physical, and, ultimately, deadly. Additionally, a neighbor has come forward. Elsa Brattenbah saw the whole thing through the front window of Captain Teague and Dr. Mallory's home as she was checking her mail at the box on the road. She will testify that Captain Teague struck Dr. Mallory with his hand. Dr. Mallory didn't simply fall and hit her head."

My heart screams as the reality of Oscar's actions comes crashing down around us all. I can see the disbelief wash over him, the shadows of regret and confusion cloaking his features.

"No ... no," he gasps, his voice hoarse as he tries to process what's happening. "That's not how it happened. I don't remember that at all."

"Evidence doesn't lie, Captain," Detective Richards continues, a steely resolve in his tone. "You need to understand that there are consequences for your actions."

As the detective says it, I remember. The feeling of Oscar striking my face. The force causing me to tumble down with such speed that I hit my head hard. I'm not sure why that had escaped my memory before, but it's there now.

Clear as day.

The courtroom holds its breath, the tension almost palpable. I watch as Oscar's world shatters and the reality of his situation sinks in. The love we shared flickers in the distance, transformed into something heavier and more complex.

And then, I find myself standing at a crossroads. Can I remain by his side, attached to someone whose choices have sealed my fate? Whose hands took the very breath from my chest?

Despair washes over me. As Oscar trembles with regret, I feel the chains of our connection weighing on my soul.

"No!" he gasps again, voice breaking, pleading. "There must be something else. I didn't hurt her! I would never hurt her!"

But even as he cries out, I sense the truth anchoring itself deeper into the fabric of this trial. Each word is a reminder of the consequences I can't escape, the choices I made in life ... and the love that twisted unexpectedly into pain.

The judge lifts her gavel, bringing the room to a hush. "Detective Richards, thank you for your testimony. We will take all of this into account as we proceed. The jury will deliberate."

As the judge speaks, I feel the walls around me begin to close in.

I stand at the precipice of our love, my being split in two. My heart draws a line deeper, and as much as I want to be there for Oscar, the undeniable truth echoes through my spirit.

It's a truth I can't escape. The reality is complicated.

The courtroom falls silent.

As the detective's words replay in my mind, I'm forced to confront the fact that our relationship was toxic. I ignored the red flags, excused the anger, and told myself that love was enough to overcome anything. It wasn't. Love didn't stop Oscar's rage from spiraling out of control. It didn't stop him from taking everything from me—my life, our future, and now, the truth of what we were.

I have to let go.

Staying connected to Oscar, hoping for a reunion in the afterlife, will only keep me bound to this pain. It's time to break free. To release the grip he has on my soul.

I loved Oscar once, with everything I had. Truly, I did. I loved him fiercely and deeply.

I can't stay with him anymore.

Not in spirit. Not in hope. Not in anything.

With one last look at my husband, I feel the final thread of our connection snap. It's time for me to move on. To find peace in whatever comes next. I'm no longer Sierra Mallory, the woman trapped by love and loyalty.

I am something more. Something that must be free.

I turn away, leaving Oscar to face the consequences of his actions. As I do, the weight of this world begins to lift. For the first time since my death, I feel a sense of release. A glimmer of the peace I've been searching for.

It's time to let go.

And so, I do.

Chapter Twenty-Four

OSCAR

When Detective Richards talked to me in the hall, he asked me if I struck my wife. I said no. I had no idea that he had such damning new evidence to prove otherwise.

How could I do something like that and not remember?

What happens next is a whirlwind as the jury deliberates for a short time before returning with a verdict. The judge's gavel swings down, and with it, my fate.

I am guilty.

Guilty of not just causing Sierra's death but of unraveling the fabric of our shared existence in a single moment of blind rage.

Faces blur around me—Sierra's parents filled with a deep sorrow, the jury reflecting a mixture of empathy and determination. I can't meet their eyes. Each glance feels like a reminder of the chasm I created.

"Captain Oscar Teague," the judge says, her voice steady but haunting. "You are hereby sentenced to fifteen years of incarceration, with eligibility for parole in ten years."

Fifteen years.

The words clang like a bell, ringing through my mind as if the walls themselves have come to bear witness to my failures. I can't breathe. I grip the edges of the table, knuckles whitening as the reality of my sentence sinks in.

Except nothing matters anymore but Sierra, and the horrible thing I did to her.

Everything slips away so quickly from my grasp. All my past achievements and all the dreams I crafted with my wife are reduced to ashes in the wake of impulse-driven madness.

"Order!" the judge barks. I can feel the air crackling with tension as the shock settles into shifting gazes. "Let's maintain decorum."

I glance to my right, where Sierra's parents sit with Beth. Their faces are stricken, shoulders hunched. Jen's lips quiver. Marty's hands are balled into tight fists. I want to tell them it will be okay and to say I'm still their son-in-law, but I'm far too ashamed.

With a nod, the officers rise, ushering me from the room. Each step feels like trudging through mud.

Denial isn't an option anymore. This path is about truth. About what I deserve.

Later, in the dim confines of my cell, I let the silence swallow me whole, suffocating and heavy, like a weight on my chest that I can never shake off. My heart feels as if it's crumbling beneath the enormity of everything that's happened.

"It's all my fault," I whisper into the void, the word tasting bitter on my tongue like an unending nightmare. "Now there's proof. She died at my hands. She was innocent and lovely. She wanted nothing but the best for me. For *us*. I took her most precious light away from this life. Away from this world and away from those who loved her. How can I go on?"

There's a point when the pain becomes unbearable. It's a tight coil that suffocates hope and joy until all I can feel is a hollowness.

I grapple with the thought of Sierra, my beautiful Sierra, forever lost. I take a shaky breath, choking back the despair that floods every corner of my being.

It's too much. Far too much.

I rise from the miniature cot, yearning for some form of relief from the torment that gnaws at me. The fluorescent lights buzz above my head, a constant reminder of the life I've wasted and the love I've irrevocably lost.

I glance towards the small window, barely visible beneath the bars. It feels like a prison not just of iron and stone, but of my own making.

The desperation unfurls into something darker and deeper—a silent call echoing in my mind. I can't bear the thought of living like this any longer. I know I'm traversing a precipice that leads to oblivion. It's the only way.

Moving decisively, I pull the bed sheet from the cot, feeling the fabric slide between my fingers like the fragmented pieces of my life. I think of the moments lost—the quiet mornings, the intimate dinners, and the shared dreams—that now dwell only in the shadowy corners of my memory.

Each moment drips with regret, and I can't allow myself to remain trapped in this shell, a ghost of the man I once was.

Is this the choice the strange man who visited me at Quantico said I'd have to make? Was he a figment of my imagination? I'm still not sure about that part, but I *am* sure about what I must do.

With a resolve born from pain, I climb toward the bars, looping the sheet with unsteady hands before securing it tightly. It's my last act of defiance against a world that feels too heavy to bear.

There is no other choice for me that makes sense.

I close my eyes, remembering the familiar warmth of Sierra enveloping me. I hold onto that memory as tightly as I can, believing that perhaps in slipping away from this life, I might find her again.

I take one final breath, and I whisper my apologies into the void.

"Sierra, I'm so sorry," I murmur. "I never meant for it to end this way."

The world blurs, dimming around me as I step into the abyss, the weight lifting from my chest, if only for a moment. I look back and see my lifeless body, hanging there, and I can't explain what I feel.

In the stillness that follows, something shifts. The darkness surrounding me dissipates and is replaced by a soft glow. I find myself standing in a vast expanse, light dancing around me like shimmering stars gliding across a velvet sky. I take a confused step forward. The air is warm and inviting, wrapping around me like a long-forgotten embrace.

And then I see her. A figure emerging from the radiant light, a silhouette I've yearned for since that fateful day when everything unraveled.

"Sierra ..." a breath catches as the awareness floods in. She stands before me, ethereal and timeless, her smile radiant and full of love. Long, flowing hair dances around her shoulders, each strand shimmering with a luminescent glow.

Is this real?

"Oscar," she whispers softly. Those two syllables carry the weight of our shared past and all the moments we cherished. I feel the warmth flood back into my being. It's a tranquility unlike anything I experienced on Earth.

"Is this ... is this heaven?" I stutter.

She shakes her head gently. "It's so much more than that. This is a realm beyond pain, beyond the darkness." Her eyes hold my gaze. "It's also a realm where love transcends both time and circumstance."

I blink back tears, overwhelmed by it all. "I'm so sorry, Sierra. I didn't mean to hurt you. I never wanted any of this."

Her expression softens, the warmth of her presence enveloping me. "I know, Oscar. I've watched you struggle. It pained me to see."

"But I'm guilty." I plead, anguish threading through my voice. "I'm responsible. I watched everything slip away. I ... hurt you."

Sierra moves closer, her gaze searching mine, and I can feel the depth of her love radiating throughout the space between us. Yet, as comforting as it is, her energy is different. She embodies a quiet determination that tells me she's reached a conclusion I dread to face.

"Oscar," she begins, her voice steady and soft. "We've both endured far too much pain. It's time to understand that love can take many forms, and sometimes, it means letting go."

"No," I plead, my voice filled with desperation. "We can fix this. We can find a way back to each other. I need you. I love you, Sierra!"

Even without my injured brain causing me to panic, I feel desperate. I just want to be with Sierra. I want to spend eternity with her. I want us to be together. I want to find a place where we can be.

Her expression shifts. "You have to understand that while love can bind us in life, it can also become a chain that holds us prisoner in death," she explains. "I cannot remain tethered to your pain. It won't heal us."

The truth in her words settles like a stone in my being. I recall every argument, the day that spiraled out of control, and the moment I lost myself completely and shattered the very essence of our bond.

"Letting go doesn't mean forgetting. It means accepting what was," she continues, her voice steadying, even as I feel the finality in her decision wash over me. "You must reclaim the essence of *you*, Oscar. You need to learn to live again without me—as painful as that may be. And I need to do the same. I'm finally ready to do the same."

"No," I whisper, trembling at the thought. "I can't do this without you. You are my heart, Sierra!"

"This connection that binds us here is keeping us from moving forward," she says. "I need to be free, just as you do. You can honor my memory without my presence, but you must be brave enough to let me go."

Tears stream down my cheeks, each drop a painful reminder of the love I've lost and the decision she's making. "Please don't do this," I plead, my voice trembling. "You're everything to me."

"I'm sorry, Oscar. It is done."

I want to scream, to yell out my anguish, but Sierra's words resonate with a truth that binds tighter around my heart.

She's right.

The love we shared shouldn't be just a painful reminder of loss. It should ignite a spark of hope that carries us both forward.

"I will always love you, Sierra," I whisper. "But I can't imagine an existence without you—in this life or the next one. You're my everything."

"You must be your own everything," she replies. "I will always be a part of you, just like you're a part of me. But it's time for both of us to move on."

As tears blur my vision, I realize I can't fight against her truth. This isn't a goodbye that ends everything. It's the promise of new beginnings that stretch across whatever lies ahead for both of us.

"Goodbye, Oscar," she says softly.

"Goodbye."

Chapter Twenty-Five

SIERRA

It's bright and sunny on the day I say farewell to this world for good.

Before I go, I take one last look at the people and places that mean the most to me. And that doesn't include Oscar. He and I are in the past. Today is about preparing for my future.

I float on the gentle breeze, feeling the warmth of the sun on my ethereal skin as I traverse the familiar path along the riverside near my childhood home in Savannah. The flowers stand proudly, blooming in all their colors, fluttering like small flags in the light wind. They're a testament to life continuing unabated. I take a moment to breathe it all in.

Memories flood back—those sun-drenched afternoons with friends, picnics by the river, laughter echoing through the trees. Each image feels alive, vibrant, as I deliberate over the beauty that once filled my heart. The essence of joy pulses around me.

For the first time in a long time, I truly feel free.

I pause beside a flowering dogwood tree, its delicate blossoms fluttering softly in the breeze. This tree was my favorite as a child. I spent countless afternoons climbing its branches, imagining it was a ship sailing me to far-away worlds.

"Goodbye, my friend," I whisper, reaching out to caress the rough bark, feeling its familiar resonance. "You taught me that even the strongest storms cannot uproot me, that I can flourish anywhere. You continue to grow, and so will I."

With an understanding nod, I step back, allowing bittersweet memories to intermingle with the new resolve blossoming within me.

Next, I glide over to my old elementary school, the walls still painted bright with the laughter of children. I remember the hopes and dreams we spun during recess and the innocent ambitions we held in our palms. That's why I wanted to work with kids as a clinical psychologist. We were souls untainted by the complexities of adulthood.

"Thank you," I murmur as I stand before its entrance. It's a place that nurtured my spirit and offered me shelter. "Thank you for helping me discover who I am, and for the lessons that will follow me through all my tomorrows."

Taking a deep breath, I inhale the fragrance of nostalgia, feeling it swirl around me, vibrant and alive.

As I traverse these halls once more, the faces of my classmates float into the air.

With each step, I feel lighter, shedding layers of grief that have clung to my spirit like a winter chill. I'm approaching closure, one that blends loss with freedom and love with acceptance.

I visit my dear parents, Beth, Brian, and even Carl and Rita. I soak up their love and friendship, feeling grateful for their presence in my life. Every minor disagreement we had is forgiven. These are people who genuinely care about me. They always have.

I drift toward the vast ocean where waves lap softly against the shore, embracing the sands in a rhythm as timeless as love itself. Here, I stand at the water's edge, letting the coolness wash over me as it mingles with the warmth of the sun above. The beach has always been one of my favorite places. Now, I feel as though I'm on the brink of something significant. A new beginning that will breathe life into the very essence of my being.

As I step toward the ocean, the waves reach back, inviting me into their embrace. I take one last glance over my shoulder, bathed in the warmth of my memories.

With a calming breath, I immerse myself in the water's depths, feeling myself dissolve into the salt and sun. The light wraps around me in a soft cocoon.

I float, and the currents embrace me, pulling me toward what lies beyond.

Finally, I am at peace.

Epilogue

Thirty Years Later

Samantha, a pretty young woman in her twenties with long, chestnut-colored hair, sits in the back row of the lecture hall at Emory University. Her notebook is open and her pen is in hand as Dr. Emanuel Harris begins today's lesson. The topic is crisis communication. It's a subject she finds both fascinating and relevant to her studies in clinical psychology.

"Today, we're going to discuss various forms of crisis communication," Dr. Harris says, turning to the whiteboard. He writes the letters *S-O-S* in bold, clear strokes. "Let's start with a classic example. Who can tell me what these letters stand for?"

Several hands shoot up, and Dr. Harris nods to a student in the front row.

"Save Our Souls," the student answers confidently.

"Correct," Dr. Harris says. "SOS is a universally recognized distress signal, originally used in maritime communications. It's a call for help. A way to signal that immediate assistance is needed. What's interesting is how this concept of SOS—of sending out a distress signal—can be applied beyond its original context."

He pauses, letting the idea sink in before continuing. "Now, some of you might be familiar with the NATO phonetic alphabet, used in various forms of communication, particularly in the military and aviation. Each letter of the alphabet is assigned a word to ensure clarity over radio transmissions. For example, *A* is *Alpha*, *B* is *Bravo*, and so on. In this system, *Sierra* represents the letter *S* and *Oscar* represents the letter *O*."

Samantha leans forward slightly, intrigued by the discussion. As she listens, she feels a strange sense of resonance with the idea of SOS—a call for help sent out into the world, often in moments of desperation.

Dr. Harris continues, "In psychological terms, an SOS can be more than just a literal distress signal. It can represent the ways people unconsciously communicate their need for help. Through their actions, their emotions, or even their silence. Recognizing these signals is crucial for us as future clinicians."

Samantha nods along.

She's always been drawn to the idea of understanding people's unspoken cries for help. The subtle signs that might go unnoticed by others are some of the most important. It's one of the reasons she's so passionate about psychology. She wants to help people find their way when they feel lost.

Dr. Harris glances around the room. "Samantha, what do you think? How can the concept of SOS be applied in our field?"

She hesitates before answering, sitting up straight and smoothing her pencil skirt. "I think in many cases, people might not even realize they're sending out an SOS. It could be through their behavior. Maybe they're withdrawing, acting out, or just not acting like themselves. Our job is to pick up on those signals and to understand that these actions might be their way of asking for help, even if they don't say it outright."

Dr. Harris smiles approvingly. "Exactly. Recognizing those signals is key to effective intervention. We must understand that SOS isn't only about asking for help. It's about survival. About finding a way through even the toughest of situations."

As the discussion moves on, Samantha can't help but feel a deep connection to the concept of SOS. It makes her think about how often people send out these silent signals, hoping someone will notice and care enough to reach out. Maybe, just maybe, it's part of her purpose to be the one who answers those calls.

The letters on the board—*Sierra Oscar Sierra*—linger in her mind, a reminder of the importance of paying attention. It's a small thing, but it feels significant. Like a lesson she's meant to learn.

The café on Eagle Row in Atlanta is the kind of place that feels like a hidden gem, even though it's always bustling with people. As Samantha walks in, the smell of fresh coffee mingles with the warm scent of pastries and the soft murmur of conversation fills the air. It's the kind of place that feels like home, even if you've never been here before.

A well-worn satchel is slung over Samantha's shoulder, brimming with books and notes. Her bright eyes scan the room. She's here for a break from her studies. To enjoy a moment of peace before diving back into her work.

As she approaches the counter, something catches her eye. A man, seated alone at a table by the window, engrossed in a book. His laptop sits open in front of him. Several stickers featuring mountain peaks are visible on the front, even from a distance. There's something about this young man—an aura of calm, of quiet strength—that draws Samantha in. She orders her coffee, but her gaze keeps drifting back to him.

When she finally gets her drink, she hesitates for a moment, then, with a small smile, she makes her way over to his table.

"Mind if I join you?" she asks.

He looks up, surprised at first, but then he smiles—a warm, genuine smile that reaches his eyes. "Not at all," he says, gesturing to the empty seat across from him. "I'm Noah."

"Samantha. Do you climb?" she asks as she sits down, nodding to the stickers.

"I'd love to, but it scares me," he explains. "I hike instead."

As they start talking, she feels an unexpected sense of ease, as if they've known each other for years. Their conversation flows effortlessly, from the books they've read to the dreams they hold for the future. He listens with an attentiveness that she's rarely encountered, and she finds herself opening up in a way that feels both natural and exhilarating.

There's a moment where she feels a deep sense of déjà vu. It's as if she's been here before. In another life, perhaps. Another time. But this time, everything feels right. There's no shadow of doubt. Just the certainty that she's exactly where she's meant to be.

Even though she might not realize it, the lessons she's learned in a life long past have shaped her into the woman she is today. Those lessons have guided her here, to this moment, where a new chapter is beginning.

THE END.

* * *

Sign up for Kelly Utt's newsletter and get the list Sierra made of everything she wants in a man PLUS private journal entries from both Sierra and Samantha.

As a subscriber, you'll be the first to get bonus content for future books, too.

Sign up at kellyutt.com!

Enjoy this book?

A note from Author Kelly Utt

Did you enjoy this book? You can make a big difference.

Honest reviews of my books help bring them to the attention of other readers.

If you've enjoyed this book, I would be very grateful if you could spend just five minutes leaving a rating or review (it can be as short as you like) on the book's retail page where you purchased and on Goodreads or BookBub.

Thank you very much.

About the Author

STANDARDS OF STARLIGHT BOOKS
KELLY UTT

Kelly Utt writes emotional, pulse-pounding suspense, family saga, and women's fiction novels. The stakes are high. The twists and turns will keep you on the edge of your seat.

Kelly was raised by a dad who would read a book, ask her to read it, too, and then insist they discuss it together, igniting her passion for life's big questions. That passion is often reflected in her novels, giving them a depth which leaves readers wanting more and thinking about her stories long after the last lines are read.

Kelly holds a Bachelor's degree in psychology from the University of Tennessee, Knoxville and a master's degree in interactive media and communications from Quinnipiac University.

She lives in Nashville, Tennessee. She also writes novels with one of her sons as the combined pen name Christopher Kelly.

www.kellyutt.com

Made in the USA
Columbia, SC
03 January 2025

48744078R00155